# The
# Sleuth's
# Miscalculation

# The Sleuth's Miscalculation

## The Librarian Sleuth—Book One

By
## Kimberly Rose Johnson

The Sleuth's Miscalculation
Published by Mountain Brook Ink
White Salmon, WA U.S.A.

Scripture quotations are taken from the King James Version of the Bible. Public domain.

© 2018 Kimberly R. Johnson
ISBN 9781-943959-39-6

The Team: Miralee Ferrell, Nikki Wright, Cindy Jackson
Cover Design: Indie Cover Design, Lynnette Bonner Designer

*Mountain Brook Ink is an inspirational publisher offering fiction you can believe in.*

Printed in the United States of America

# Dedication

*The Sleuth's Miscalculation* is dedicated to my Facebook Readers Group. I love how this group is always ready with ideas when I get stuck, as well as how encouraging this group is. You are all such a blessing to me. Thank you!

# Acknowledgments

I like to give special thanks to my critique group for their enthusiasm for this project as well as for their excellent critiquing. I don't know what I'd do without you ladies. You rock! And thanks as well to my publisher for diving into a new series with me.

# Chapter One

"Shh." Nancy Daley touched a finger to her lips and flashed her serious librarian look at the boys giggling at the computer, then hid her face behind a book. It wouldn't do to let the boys see her easy-going side. She smiled at the ridiculous thought—everyone knew she was a softy with a heart for anyone in need.

Her cell vibrated inside her desk drawer. She pulled it out. "Hi, Mom." She turned her back to the boys and kept her voice low.

"I wanted to let you know I need to cancel dinner tonight."

Nancy frowned. Although her mom was the county sheriff as well as the contracted law enforcement for the town, she rarely missed their weekly dinner. "Is everything okay?"

"Yes. I'm staying late to meet with the deputy I appointed to replace Frank."

Nancy sighed. "Is that really necessary?" Her shoulders tightened.

"We've been short staffed for months. I don't have a choice. This man was a detective in L.A., and we could use someone with his experience. As for the meeting being this evening, I had a full day and needed to reschedule for five."

"I understand." It was her fault that her mom had to find someone to replace Frank. If not for her giving him bad intel, he never would have been on the road and killed by a drunk driver. Her heart still ached from the loss.

The older man was like the father she wished she'd had, but in reality, he had simply been a good family friend and an excellent deputy. Thinking about his death still made her stomach hurt and her eyes burn. "Then I'll see you when I see you."

"Thanks for understanding. Is anything exciting going on at the library?"

Nancy turned and looked around the small one-room space with exposed brick walls, blue concrete floors, and rows of shelves, which covered two-thirds of the quirky floor space. "Everything is quiet."

"Good. See you later."

Nancy stuffed the phone back in the drawer, unable to shake the sadness thoughts of Frank had brought on. No matter how efficient or multi-talented the man her mom hired was, he'd never come close to replacing Frank.

Closing time. She stood and strolled through the aisles, checking for anything or anyone out of order. Her heels clicked on the concrete flooring. The comfort of home sounded good. She couldn't wait to change into jeans and tennis shoes.

A Nancy Drew book sat at the end of a stack. Gliding her hand across the worn cover of her childhood favorite book, she paused before sliding it into place. This series had helped her through many boring summers, and to this day, she aspired to be like the amateur sleuth.

Altering her course, she approached the computer and shut it down. The boys must have skittered away while she talked with her mom. Grabbing her purse and phone, she flicked off the lights and headed outside.

"Nancy!" Her neighbor ran up the cobblestone steps, waving. "Help." Anna Plum stopped on the top stair and bent at the waist, gasping for air. Her auburn hair fell loose around her face.

"What's wrong?" Her neighbor, a local high school English teacher looked ready to burst into tears.

"Freddy ran off." Anna's voice caught. "If Ben sees my baby loose one more time, he's going to cite me."

"Ben with Animal Control?"

She nodded. Her eyes pleaded with Nancy to hurry. The three-year-old miniature American Eskimo dog escaped at every possible chance. "I tried to catch him." She took a deep breath then let it out in a huff. "That dog is too fast. Can you help me find him? Please? Freddy loves you, and I know once you catch up to him he'll come to you if you call him especially since you always have doggie treats at hand. I sure wish he didn't enjoy being chased. It's exhausting, and he won't come to me, even for treats until he's tired of the game."

Nancy shielded her eyes to the afternoon sun. "Which way did he go?"

"Toward the town square park. He's probably there right now, but I don't think I can take another step. I ran all the way from my house, and I'm not a runner." The thirty-something woman sunk to the cobblestones and rested her elbows on her knees. "I need to catch my breath then I'll follow."

Nancy stifled a giggle. "Okay. I'll do my best to catch the rascal." Anna had her quirks, but Nancy liked the happy-go-lucky woman. Most in town felt sorry for Anna since she'd been jilted at the altar ten years ago, but Nancy didn't. Her neighbor was content to be single and put all her energy into her students. A man wasn't necessary for a complete life. Her mother married right out of high school, became pregnant with her soon after, and then Nancy's father took off when she was six-years-old, never to be heard from again.

She picked up her pace to a fast walk being careful not to twist her ankle. She never should have worn heels to work.

"Hi, Miss Daley." An eight-year-old boy from her church waved.

"Hi, Justin. Have you seen Miss Plum's dog, Freddy?"

"Sure. The kids are playing with him in the park. See you." He turned and skipped off.

"Thanks," Nancy called after him. She rounded the corner, and in the center of the town square's small park, Freddy romped with a group of children on the grass while the new play equipment stood vacant. The town should have requested a dog from the local philanthropist who donated the new equipment. It would have been cheaper and apparently more entertaining.

A teen she didn't recognize tossed a tennis ball, and the dog charged after it. Shaking her head, Nancy walked onto the grass. Her heels sank. Now more than ever she regretted her shoe choice. "Come, Freddy," she said firmly and loudly.

The white dog rolled to a stop and altered course, charging toward her. "Oh no." She braced herself. Freddy leaped into her outstretched arms, and Nancy went down. The twenty-pound dog lavished kisses on Nancy's cheek. "Okay, that's enough." She held the dog close, feeling water seep through her skirt. Of course it had rained earlier, leaving the park a bog.

A man's chuckle drew her attention. She glared at him.

"Sorry. I didn't mean to laugh." He offered his hand, which she ignored. "Is that your dog?"

Nancy looked up, shielding her eyes with the palm of her hand while maintaining control of Freddy. All six feet of the man looked down at her. A halo of light framed his handsome face. She always did enjoy a five o'clock shadow, and he knew how to wear one.

"Uh, no. He belongs to my neighbor. I'm Nancy. Thanks for the offer, but I'm good." She pushed to her knees while still cradling Freddy in one arm and stood as gracefully as possible given her pencil skirt. "Are you new in town or passing through?"

"New."

He didn't offer his name, which struck her as rude, but she shook off the slight. His cerulean blue eyes reminded her of the now cloudless sky overhead, and his dark hair shined in the sunlight.

"Gavin, it's time to go," the man said in a firm voice.

The same young teen who'd been throwing the ball jogged toward them.

"Well, it was nice meeting you." She turned and tiptoed off the grass holding tight to Freddy, who seriously needed a bath, then strolled back toward the library.

"You found him." Anna rushed toward Nancy.

Freddy wiggled in her arms and whined. Nancy held the dog tighter. "What's the matter with you? Don't you want to go home?"

Anna reached out and drew Freddy into her arms. "You gave Mama a scare, precious. No more playing chase." She smiled. "Thanks for the help, Nancy. I knew I could count on you." Her eyes widened, and her mouth formed an O as she stared at Nancy's top. "I'm so sorry about your clothes. I'll have them cleaned for you."

Nancy waved a hand. She didn't mind doing laundry. They walked side-by-side toward the library. "Don't worry about it. Would you like a ride home?" It was less than a mile to their street from where she'd parked, but she knew better than to walk to work in heels. Granted she could have changed out of her shoes, but she never could get herself to wear tennis shoes with a skirt—that might change after today though. Her shoes were probably ruined. She cringed thinking about it. Her favorite college professor's admonishment to always dress professionally stuck with her to a fault.

"Thanks. That would be nice."

Nancy grabbed an old towel she kept for times like these. She spread the towel on her seat then slid behind the wheel and buckled up while Anna got situated with her dog. "I met a man who is new to town at the park. He was there with a young teen boy—I'm guessing fourteen, maybe fifteen, whom I assume was his son. They were playing with your dog."

"We can always use a fresh face around here." Anna waggled her brows. "Is he a looker?"

Nancy did a double-take in her neighbor's direction and held in her laughter. She'd never seen Anna waggle her brows like that. "He's not bad. But like you, I'm not in the market for a man. Men are trouble."

"Don't judge all men by your dad."

"I'm not. Look what happened to you."

"Least of all, don't judge men based on my experience. Sam did me a favor not showing up that day." Anna chuckled. "Although it didn't feel like it at the time or for a long while after."

"I don't understand how you can always be so happy. Most women would be bitter and hate men after what Sam did to you."

"I was serious when I said he did me a favor. Although, I wish he'd realized we weren't meant to be together sooner, I find the situation humorous. I mean, really. The high school English teacher is jilted at the altar—it's so cliché." Anna shrugged. "I'll admit to being a little shy now when it comes to men, but I have a full life, and I'm happy—if only this rascal dog would behave." She clicked her tongue. "Not all men are cowards and undependable, Nancy."

No, only the ones that counted.

Carter sat in one of several empty chairs. He looked around the Sheriff's office reception area and adjusted his tie for the umpteenth time. His meeting was slated for five o'clock. It was now five-fifteen. He'd left Gavin at the pizza joint around the corner with a pocketful of quarters to play in the small arcade. At fifteen, Gavin was smarter than average and knew how to stay out of trouble, but trouble often found him. Hopefully the quarters would keep him entertained, and he'd be there waiting when this interview was over.

The door that led to the back office creaked. "Mr. Malone?" A middle-aged woman who stood around five-foot-eight inches approached him. Her hair was pulled into a ponytail, and her broad shoulders filled out her brown uniform. There was something familiar about her, but he couldn't quite place why.

He jumped up. "Yes."

She offered her hand. "I'm Sheriff Daley. It's nice to meet you in person." She turned and walked past two desks. "I'm sorry for keeping you waiting. Even in this small town, things come up." She glanced over her shoulder before entering an office with a window facing into the interior as well as an exterior window that faced an alley—crummy view.

At least his future boss could see out. He always liked being able to see outside because it made him feel less hemmed in.

"I understand." He'd been living in L.A. for years and had few memories of small town life. If she said things came up then they must. Since arriving in Tipton earlier today, the only violation he'd spotted was a dog running free in the town square park. Which was fine by him. His two years with the L.A. police department had provided enough excitement to last a lifetime.

"I'm curious why you want to work here. Don't get me wrong, I'm pleased to have you. Your skills will be put to great use, but surely you have more lucrative opportunities in California. I can't imagine why you'd want to work in a small Oregon town."

"I recently adopted my teen-aged nephew and getting out of the rat race appeals to me. This seems like a nice place to raise him."

"It is. I raised my daughter here, and she turned out great." A broad smile lit her face.

Thirty minutes later Carter stood and shook his new boss's hand. "Thanks, Sheriff Daley. I'll be here first thing Monday morning." He pocketed his badge and scooped up his uniform.

"See that you're on time. I have zero tolerance for

tardiness. Oh, and keep an eye out for any suspicious activity around parked vehicles."

He raised a brow. "Something going on?"

"It's the strangest thing. A couple of cars have had their plates stolen today. If that's not odd enough, only the back plate is missing. Good thing Oregon uses both front and back plates." She shook her head.

He rubbed his chin. "I'll keep my eyes open." He nodded then rapidly retraced his steps. The clock on the wall said six. Gavin's quarters probably ran out a while ago. He pushed into Maggie's Pizza and spotted the teen at a booth along the side wall with a soda in hand, playing on his phone. "Hey, how'd it go?" He bumped fists with his nephew and slid in across from him.

Gavin shrugged and went back to his game. "I'm hungry. Can we get a pizza?"

"Great idea. Cheese?"

Gavin nodded without looking up.

"Be right back." He approached the counter and stood in line behind the same woman he'd seen at the park earlier. A smile touched his lips at the memory. She'd been a sight with grass and mud on her curvy bare legs and a huge wet grass stain on her backside. Whoever owned the dog she retrieved owed her big time.

Now, her long chestnut hair was pulled back in clips on the sides, and she wore jeans and a pale blue top. She'd traded the heels for practical navy sneakers. She moved forward in line and ordered a small Canadian bacon and pineapple with extra cheese. When finished, she turned with her head down looking into her purse and rammed into him. "Oh, excuse me." Recognition shone in her eyes, then they shuttered. "Hello again."

"Nancy, right?"

She nodded.

He thrust out his hand. "Carter. Sorry I didn't introduce myself earlier. I was pre-occupied because I had to meet with my new boss." Truth was he'd been nervous about meeting the Sheriff and regretted his lack of decorum.

She took his hand hesitantly. "Nice to meet you, Carter. Did your meeting go well?"

"Yes. I start Monday."

"What do you do?"

"I'm a deputy with the Sheriff's Department."

"Next." The cashier spoke with an annoyed look on his face.

"Guess that's me."

She stepped aside allowing him to place his order.

"Are you getting it to go?" Carter asked.

She nodded.

He pocketed his change the cashier gave him and pivoted toward her. "I'm glad to see someone besides us in here. It's always a bad sign when no one frequents a restaurant."

"I never thought about it, but I see how that would be true. Maggie serves the best pizza in Tipton."

"I was under the impression it was the only pizza place. Is there another?"

She smirked and shook her head. "Have you found a place to live yet?"

"No. Any suggestions? We're staying at a local bed and breakfast right now. I'm hoping to buy, but we need a place sooner rather than later."

"Lucky for you I rarely clean out my purse." She dug around. "Here it is." She pulled a card from her purse and wrote an address. It's vacant and a nice little place with good bones. If it suits you, give the real estate agent on the other side a call. From what I've been told, Lilly Prescott is great to work with."

"Thanks." He slipped the card into his shirt pocket, then sauntered to where his nephew waited.

"Wasn't that the lady with the dog?" Gavin motioned toward where Nancy had been standing a moment ago.

"Yes, it was. How about you put your phone away for now?"

"In a minute. I'm almost to the next level."

Carter let his mind wander to everything that had to be done by Monday. Three days! Too bad it was already dark outside or he'd take a look at the house tonight. "Guess what?"

"Hmm?" Gavin stuffed the phone into his jeans pocket.

"I start my new job Monday. We should get you enrolled in school tomorrow, and I need to find us a place to live fast so we can return the U-Haul on Sunday."

"But today is Thursday. How are you going to find us a place to live and move in by Sunday?"

His nephew had a valid question, but failure wasn't an option. "I already have a lead on a vacant house. We can move in fast if we work together." Assuming he could work out some kind of arrangement with the owners. Their order was announced, and he stood, noting that Nancy had left. He should've invited her to join them, but he was sure to run into her again, at least he hoped so. She seemed like a nice person. After all, she rescued pets and the homeless.

He placed the tray on the table. "Eat up. The bed and breakfast doesn't have a refrigerator." He still couldn't believe the only hotel in town was under renovation and what rooms they had were booked. At least the manager had directed him to a nice B and B.

Gavin inhaled half the pizza without taking a break for conversation, then patted his stomach and burped.

"Excuse you."

His nephew shot him a sheepish look. "I met a couple of guys in the arcade room. They invited me to hang out with them at the skate park on Saturday. Can I?"

"I'll think about it. It will all depend on how fast we find a place and get settled." On top of that he didn't want his nephew associating with the wrong crowd. That was one of the reasons he'd moved them to the middle of nowhere. He could probably spare an hour and accompany Gavin to the park, but it would be tight with all he had to accomplish.

"Come on, Uncle Carter. My dad would let me. I need friends, and I liked these guys. They said they'd be skateboarding in the park tomorrow after school too."

His younger brother, Gavin's dad, was not a stellar example of good parenting. Although skateboarding sounded harmless enough, he'd be more comfortable accompanying his nephew. "Like I said, we have a lot to do, but I imagine an hour break would be a good idea."

"You don't have to be there. I'm not a baby. You could keep working."

"Not happening." Carter stood. "Don't worry, they'll never know we're together."

"But—"

"Either we both go, or neither go. Your choice. You ready?"

"Yeah." Gavin stood but didn't look happy.

They walked side-by-side out the door and then several blocks to the B and B. He noted a florist, coffee shop, pet store, bookstore, bakery, and drug store as they walked along the tree-lined sidewalk. All of which were closed except the coffee shop.

Tires squealed. He whipped around to see a late model Chevy race around the corner. Must be teens out joy riding—but on a Thursday night? His stomach knotted.

The same car fish-tailed down the block in front of them and headed right for them. He pushed his nephew into the entryway of a store and plastered his body to the building as the car zoomed past, nearly jumping the curb. Had he made a mistake coming to this small town where whatever happened was sure to have an impact on his nephew?

# Chapter Two

GAZING OUT HER KITCHEN WINDOW, NANCY moved the phone away from her ear as her over-excited friend Gloria emoted. "I know it's crazy, but I'm desperate. You have to help me. Think of it as an adventure. It's not every day you're given permission to break into a home. I can't leave the park with ten of my daughter's friends here and no other adults stuck around. It's her fifth birthday. Please, Nancy." Gloria's voice came across as a whine. "I don't know who else to call. I've tried everyone I can think of, and they're all busy."

"Okay. I understand." She kept her voice calm and soothing. "But, are you sure you want me to break a window to get inside? There isn't a key hidden anywhere? Or I could pop over to the park and get your house key."

"No. That will take too long. These kids expect cupcakes, and they'll turn violent if I don't deliver."

"Do you have any idea how expensive it is to replace a window?"

"Sweetie, do I sound like I care? Money isn't an issue, and it won't be the first time I've had to break the tiny window to open the door. The glass company and I know each other by now."

Nancy's eyes widened. This was nuts. She knew Gloria had money, but this was a little over the top.

"The histrionics my five-year-old will go into once she realizes her cupcakes aren't here are worth any price to avoid. Please hurry."

Nancy stifled a giggle at the woman's exaggeration. Then again, she'd witnessed the child's tantrums, and they were not a laughing matter. "I could stop by the bakery and pick up a dozen cupcakes, my treat."

"No! Elsa is allergic to so many things; I can't risk a hospital visit. Besides, I made her favorite recipe."

Her shoulders sagged. "Okay. I'll do it, but I'm not comfortable with this."

"Noted. Just get here!"

Nancy slipped on flip-flops then thought better of it. If she'd be walking through broken glass, she'd need real shoes. A minute later she ran out the door and slid behind the wheel of her blue Mustang, threw it into gear, and hit the gas. Her tires squealed as she rocketed forward.

The car roared beneath her as she screeched around the corner and zipped up the next block. Good thing her mom was the sheriff. Two minutes later, she parked in front of Gloria's ranch-style house. The Victorian bed and breakfast that the new guy was staying in next door was beautiful. Painted in period-colors and with a wrap-around porch it begged you to come in and sit in one of the old-fashioned rockers. Gloria's newer home was immaculately landscaped and well-kept, but the Victorian's grandeur made her friend's house look dismal in comparison.

Nancy hopped out and jogged along the side of the house into the back yard. This was crazy, and she knew it, but she couldn't leave Gloria to the wrath of ten five-year-olds, or risk little Elsa going to the hospital if she accidentally ate something she was allergic to. She looked around her friend's perfectly manicured yard.

"What exactly am I supposed to break the window with?" The yard was child proof.

With a sigh, she ran back to her car, grabbed the towel she kept in the trunk for those just-in-case times, then hustled back to the door. She wrapped the towel around her forearm making sure to cover her elbow with several layers, then with one quick elbow to the pane it broke. Shattering glass smashed to the ground. Carefully, so as to avoid the sharp, jagged edges she reached in and unlocked the door, and then stepped across the glass crunching beneath her sneakers.

Cupcakes sat on the counter. All two-dozen decorated in pink frosting with large princess stickers stuck to the paper holders.

"Hold it!"

Nancy whirled around and screamed. She focused on the gun in his hand pointed at her. "What are you doing?" The new deputy her mom hired looked like he meant business. Her heart pounded. "Easy now. I have permission to be here."

"Raise your hands where I can see them."

Her stomach lurched. "Are you serious? We met in the park and then again at Maggie's Pizza, remember? I rescued my neighbor's dog. Surely you don't think—"

"I said raise your hands."

Her stomach lurched at the menacing sound in his voice. Her arms shot up of their own accord. "Call Gloria. This is her place. She asked me to pick up these cupcakes for her daughter's party in the park." This was the last thing she'd expected to happen. At least she knew her mom had hired a good deputy—too good from her perspective.

"I suppose she asked you to break her window—"

"Yes! Now will you please put that thing away, before someone gets hurt?" Unease skittered up her spine. She'd grown up around guns, but having one pointed at her was an entirely different thing.

"You're under arrest."

"For what?" This couldn't be happening.

"For breaking and entering. You have the right to remain silent. Anything you say can and will be used against you in a court of law."

Nancy tuned out the familiar spiel and was startled when he slapped cuffs on her wrists. At least he'd kept her hands in front of her. "You're kidding me! Do you know who I am?"

"You have any I.D.?"

"Yes, of course. It's in my purse." She dipped her chin. "Which is at home on my kitchen counter."

He guided her out the door. "Save it for the judge."

"This can all be cleared up, if you'd talk to Gloria." She grimaced at the desperation in her voice. "She's the home owner."

"Oh, I will, but I'm booking you first. Is that your Mustang, or did you steal it?"

"It's mine." She squared her shoulders. "You're going to regret this, Carter."

"It's Deputy Malone. I'm off duty, so we'll have to take my car to the station."

More likely he hadn't officially started working. "Please! Contact Gloria. Her number is on my cell phone. This is her house, and she'll vouch for me. You really don't need to do this."

She gritted her teeth at his silence. Clearly, he wasn't afraid she was a dangerous criminal, or he wouldn't transport her in his own vehicle. Was that even legal? "Wait!" She stopped moving. "If you call 911 and have one of the deputies come over, I'll be cleared. I'm sure of it." As soon as they saw what was going on they'd release her, and she could get those cupcakes to the park.

"No can do. I'm not pulling them away from a legit potential emergency." He guided them out of the house and to the curb. He opened the passenger door to his black Dodge Dart. "Get in. And don't try anything."

"Do you really think I'm stupid enough to break into a house that has a bed and breakfast filled with guests right next door?"

"You just did. And thanks for the tip about the house for sale. My nephew and I move in tomorrow. Our offer was accepted, so the owners are letting us rent while we wait for escrow to close."

"Congratulations." She wrinkled her nose and slid in.

He ran around the front of the car and sat beside her.

"I like your car." She couldn't blame him for arresting her since he didn't really know her. Gloria was probably frantic about those cupcakes. "Do you think we could swing by the park on the way to the station?"

He cast a sideways glance in her direction as the engine purred to life. "Why?"

"I told you Gloria is expecting me to show up with the cupcakes."

A look of doubt clouded his blue eyes. He shook his head. "The only place you're going to is jail." He muttered something about small towns.

Five minutes later, they parked at the county courthouse where the Tipton Sheriff's Office was housed.

"Stay put. I'll be around to get the door."

"You're sure bossy." She flipped her head, causing her long hair to move out of her face. The door opened, and she stepped out.

"After you." He motioned for her to walk inside.

She rolled her eyes, and with her chin held high strode through the courthouse and into the sheriff's office where there were three holding cells. The moment she walked in, the normal buzz silenced.

"This way." He guided her to booking.

"I want to speak to the sheriff."

"She's busy," Carter said.

"Afternoon, Lyle." Nancy nodded at the long-time deputy and department chief who sat behind his desk typing on his laptop.

"Nancy." Surprise lit his face when his gaze landed on her cuffed wrists.

"Is the sheriff around?" She asked.

"Out. Looks like you've met Deputy Malone." Lyle stood. "What'd you do?"

"Nothing!"

"I caught this woman breaking into the neighbor's house beside the bed and breakfast where I'm staying. She claims to have permission to be there, but she broke the window on the back door to get inside."

"It's Gloria Davis's place," Nancy said.

A knowing look filled Lyle's eyes as he nodded. "Did you check with the homeowner to confirm Nancy's story?"

"No, not yet, but who in her right mind would ask someone to break a window that will easily cost over a hundred dollars to replace?"

"You haven't met Gloria or her little girl. Both are in their right minds but more than a little high strung and impulsive. As for Nancy..." Lyle crossed his arms over his chest and chuckled. "Do you have any idea who you've arrested?"

"Why do people keep asking me that?" Carter muttered. "Where I come from the law is the law no matter who the person is, unless said person has diplomatic immunity."

"Give it a rest, cowboy. I didn't break and enter as you assumed. If you'd call the homeowner, this could be cleared up in seconds. Her number is in my cell phone."

Nancy looked around the small space that housed the sheriff's department and noticed two sets of smiling eyes watching from the conference room. Why wasn't anyone making him let her go? "Will one of you please tell him to set me free?" How could they stand there doing nothing? "This isn't funny! And these cuffs hurt."

Lyle sobered. "Oh. Sorry 'bout that, Nancy." He pulled out a set of keys and freed her hands.

She rubbed her wrists and glared at her would-be captor. "You!" Words escaped her as the events of the past twenty minutes set in.

Deputy Malone stood slack jawed. "What's going on here? I caught her red handed breaking and entering."

"Carter Malone, meet Nancy Daley. Sheriff Daley's daughter. If she said she had permission, then she did. This lady is as honest as they come." The balding chief eyed Nancy. "What was so important she had you break into her house?"

"Cupcakes. Elsa's birthday." Her stomach niggled at Lyle's proclamation. She hadn't always been the honest person she was now. At a young age she'd learned the hard way the cost of a lie.

Lyle busted up laughing. "I've heard it all. That's great. Malone, get the number from Nancy and call Gloria to let her know what happened, then maybe you could help deliver those cupcakes."

He couldn't have heard correctly. "You're releasing her? And you want me to help with cupcakes?" He knew things were more lax in Tipton, Oregon, but even for a small town, this seemed ridiculous.

Nancy handed him her cell phone. "It's ringing, and it's for you."

He hesitated and took the phone. "Hello?"

"Nancy, where are you?" A frantic woman who sounded near tears shouted into the phone.

"This is Deputy Malone with the Tipton County Sheriff's Office. Miss Daley was arrested for breaking and entering your home, ma'am." She screeched something he couldn't understand. Was the woman crying or laughing? He pulled the phone away from his ear and handed it back to Nancy. "I think we better hurry with those cupcakes. She sounds ready to break."

Nancy glared at him and grabbed the phone as she rushed out the door. "Calm down, Gloria. We're on our way." She tilted her head toward Carter. "You really shouldn't have crossed Gloria. She's a big financial supporter of the park. If it weren't for her, this town wouldn't have the new play equipment."

He hadn't even officially started work, and he'd already alienated the boss's daughter and a philanthropic citizen. If word got out about this, he'd be the laughing stock of Tipton—again. Well, maybe no one was laughing back then, but they sure had believed the worst. At least no one remembered him from his short stint living here so long ago. He tossed Nancy the keys. "You drive." Most of his memories from his stay here as a child were foggy—he only had one strong memory and he'd rather forget it. Maybe he'd met Sheriff Daley when he was a kid and that's why she seemed familiar.

"Seriously? You trust me with your car?"

"Call it an act of good faith or an apology. You know your way around town better than me, and I have a feeling Gloria has reached her limit."

"Enough said." She pulled out of the parking lot and whipped down a street he hadn't yet discovered. In a matter of minutes, they were parked outside the bed and breakfast. "I'll take it from here, deputy."

She ran alongside the house and a minute later slid into her Mustang and tore away. Curious about this Gloria woman and more than a little concerned for her sanity, he followed Nancy. He had to give her credit for being a good friend.

He parked a few spots behind Nancy and watched as she hustled the cupcake platter toward a group of young children. The kids spotted her and charged her direction. *Whoa.* Those kids were out of control. Time to make up for earlier. He grabbed a duffle bag off the back seat and raced her direction, unzipping his bag and pulling out a few balloons. Making balloon animals had been a hobby for as long as he could remember. It helped him to relax and he always kept a handful of balloons in his duffle. "Hey kids! Who wants a balloon hat?" He dropped the bag at his feet

"Me! Me!" One little girl wearing purple pants and a black hoodie raised her hand and hopped up and down.

Nancy shot him a look that seemed to say, 'thanks, but you're nuts.' How could a single look say so much? She moved over to the table where a frazzled woman stood looking their direction.

The kids crowded around him as he made a pink elephant hat and then a purple bug with antennas. Before long, the ladies were gathering the children to the table.

Nancy sidled up to him. "Thanks. That was a nice distraction, so we could get the cupcakes set out."

"You're welcome. I figured it was the least I could do...considering."

"True. You're good at making those. I once knew a boy who loved making balloon shapes."

"A kid? That's different."

"Yeah. So was he. A good kind of different," she quickly added wistfully. "See you around." She waved to Gloria before leaving.

Carter sauntered to his car. He really shouldn't have left Gavin for so long, especially since he'd promised he'd take him skateboarding with the kids he'd met at the pizza place. He glanced at his watch and groaned. He'd busted Nancy right as he and Gavin were preparing to head to the park. His nephew would be steaming by now.

A familiar laugh grabbed his attention. He turned. "Gavin?" His nephew hopped a curb on his skateboard, shot past him and kept going. At least he wore a helmet and wrist guards. The teen had wiped out last year and broken his wrist—he must not want a repeat event.

His cell phone rang. "This is Carter."

"Sheriff Daley here. If you're free, I'd like you to come to the office. We need to talk."

His stomach sank. Everyone who worked for the sheriff served at her whim. He'd been warned there would be no job security here, but he never imagined getting fired before he officially started. "I'll be right over."

He sent Gavin a text telling him he'd meet him at the B and B later, then he left. It looked like his nephew was getting what he wanted after all—freedom. There was nothing he could do about it at the moment. He'd be sure to sit Gavin down later and spell out the house rules. Taking off without checking in first was not okay. Then again, he'd done the same thing to his nephew. It would have to go both ways for sure.

After a few wrong turns Carter pulled up to the courthouse and sat in his car, hoping he wasn't going to get fired. He'd only been in town a few days, yet the place and the people had grown on him once again. He didn't want to leave—plus he needed stability for Gavin. *Lord, I could use an intervention. You know my heart. Please help this job to work out.*

The back door to the courthouse swung open, and Lyle strode out. He motioned for Carter to put down his window. "What are you doing?"

"Praying."

Lyle nodded. "I knew I liked you. Even if you did run in the sheriff's daughter."

"About that. How angry is she?"

Lyle shrugged.

"Okay. Guess I'd better get in there before she calls again." He got out, and squared his shoulders. "Here goes nothing."

Lyle chuckled and gave him a friendly slap on the back. "Glad I'm not you."

"Thanks," he said dryly.

As Carter stepped inside, all eyes riveted on him. He knocked on his boss's door and pushed in when she said to enter. His eyes widened when he spotted Nancy sitting opposite her mother. "Ma'am." He greeted his boss.

"Glad you were free. I know it's not yet Monday, but seeing as you are so eager to jump into the job, I thought I'd give you something to chew on while you get settled."

"About that. I had no idea Nancy is your daughter."

Sheriff Daley waved a hand as if it didn't matter. "Let it go, Carter. I have something more important, and I want you to work with Nancy on this."

"Excuse me?"

"Nancy is clever and perceptive. We sometimes use her as a behind-the-scenes consultant to help with less violent crimes."

"And the powers that be don't think that's an ethics issue?"

The sheriff's eyes narrowed. "Nancy has proven herself many times, and although she deserves to be paid, it's not in the budget. She volunteers her time. Besides that, we keep what she does for us quiet. There's no reason to put a target on her back."

"Oh." Maybe it was time he shut his mouth and listened.

"I believe I mentioned to you the other night about license plates being stolen off vehicles."

He nodded and avoided looking Nancy's direction, unsure how he felt about the county using a civilian.

"It's happening county-wide, not only here in town. As you know, the city contracts with us for police protection via our deputies so we're it. You'll report to Lyle and myself for this case. Got it?"

"Yes, Ma'am." He'd heard of small towns choosing to contract the sheriff's office for police protection in lieu of hiring their own police force, but this was his first experience serving in that capacity.

She filled him in on the details. "Use Nancy to get acquainted with the town's residents. She knows almost everyone." She cast a proud look toward her daughter. "I know it's not necessary to tell *you* this, Carter, but Nancy, be careful. We don't know whom we're up against. This could be kids pulling a prank, or we could be dealing with something bigger."

"Mom, don't worry. I'm good at keeping below the radar. Besides, no one knows I consult for law enforcement except those who need to know, and they are discreet. And before I forget, thanks for the ride to the station. I'd probably still be hoofing it back to my car if you hadn't happened along." Nancy stood, sent Carter a look he couldn't read, and left the room.

Sheriff Daley laughed. "Word to the wise. Don't underestimate my daughter. See you Monday."

Carter nodded. For the first time he wondered if moving to Tipton had been a mistake. What had he gotten himself into?

# Chapter Three

SUNDAY AFTERNOON CARTER PUSHED HIS BROWN leather sofa into place along the wall and stepped back. Not bad. The bungalow that Nancy recommended had turned out to be the perfect fit for him and Gavin. Though small, the place felt cozy and lived-in, which he liked.

He turned and glanced out the front window. Sunshine filtered through clouds, lighting the small manicured lawn and mature shrubs. A blue Mustang stopped along the curb, and Nancy stepped out—right on time. He'd invited her over to discuss the license plate case, so that she wouldn't be spending an unusual amount of time at the sheriff's office. Besides, he didn't mind meeting with her on his off time. If he was going to survive in this town as a law enforcement officer, he had to make nice with the boss's daughter no matter how much he disagreed with involving a civilian in police business.

Nancy strode up the concrete walkway. She wore black knee-high boots over jeans that hugged her shapely legs, and a long black sweater hung past her hips. How could she possibly work undercover when she looked that good? Every single man in town must have a crush on the wannabe sleuth.

A knock sounded. He ambled to the door, squared his shoulders, then pulled it open. His heart skidded. She looked even better up close. He stood in the doorway with a hand resting on the door.

Nancy blinked doe-like brown eyes. "Is something wrong? Do I have chocolate on my face?" She brushed the back of her hand across her mouth. "Dark chocolate is my vice. I eat it whenever I'm stressed—or happy. My mood doesn't matter."

He held back a chuckle and stepped aside, allowing her to enter. "Which one are you today? Stressed or happy?"

A tiny grin tipped her lips. "Both." She pulled an open chocolate bar from her oversized purse. "Would you like a square?" She broke off a piece and popped it into her mouth. No wonder she was worried about chocolate on her face. She had a hard time keeping her lips closed around the confection.

"I'm good, but thanks." This vulnerability was a side to the independent woman he hadn't expected. He led her into the family room with the brown couch. "I thought we could talk in here."

Nancy sat in the recliner that faced the couch. "I'm impressed with how fast you moved in."

"Gavin was a big help, and it was pretty easy since we only have the basics. I returned the U-Haul a little while ago."

She glanced around the space, admiration in her eyes. "It looks like your stuff was made for this place."

"Thanks. Gavin and I thought the same thing." He eased onto the couch and pulled out his notepad and pen. "Before we begin, I'd like to clear the air between us. I'm hoping we can move past what went down at Gloria's."

"I'd like that."

"Good. Me too." A weight lifted from his shoulders. "When do you think you can introduce me to the business owners?"

She frowned. "I don't know if my mom's idea was so great. Under normal circumstances, taking you around with me would be fine, but with us working this case together, I wonder if people will suspect something."

He almost laughed but coughed to cover it. "That's probably the best reason for you showing me around. We'd throw off any possible suspicion—it'd be too obvious."

"Hmm. You make a valid point. But, I wouldn't want anyone to think we're a couple either."

He chuckled.

"Why is that funny?"

"Why would anyone assume we're a couple simply because you are showing me around?"

"Have you ever lived in a small town before?"

"Actually, I have, but I was a kid."

"Then you were too young to understand. Now that I think about it, it's common for me to show people around. I seem to be the welcome committee of one in Tipton."

He tucked that information aside and focused on the distant look in her eyes. What was she thinking about? And why did she seem sad? He cleared his throat. "I suppose we should discuss the case. Do you have any new information?"

She crossed one leg over her knee. "Nothing new. I figured since we were working this together, I'd wait for your lead. You are, after all, the professional, and I'm only an amateur."

"Thank you." Her cooperation surprised and pleased him. He expected her to run ahead and get herself into trouble as she had when she broke into Gloria's house.

Maybe Nancy had a rational side. He flipped to the page with his recent notes on the case. "There was another missing license plate reported over the weekend. It happened Saturday afternoon. The vehicle—a 1991 F150—was parked on Front Street. When the owner returned, she noticed the plate missing."

"Is she certain it happened yesterday?" Nancy pulled a laptop from her bag and opened it. "I charted the locations of all the thefts inside the city limits on a map." She pressed a few buttons then stood and handed him the laptop. "As you can see, they all took place in the downtown area."

"Right." This information wasn't new to him, but he wondered why Nancy felt the need to point it out. Was she trying to prove herself? "You mentioned you're stressed. Any particular reason? Is this case a problem?"

"No. But..." She glanced around the room as if looking for the answer to his question. She took her laptop from him and returned to the recliner. "You seem like a man who appreciates honesty, so I'm going to put this out there. When Mom told me she wanted us on this case together, I fought her, but she persisted. I don't want to work with a partner, but I trust my mom's judgment. For whatever reason, she believes we need to do this together. I know we agreed to start over, but you should know that before we cleared the air, I was stressed about coming here. You're not my favorite person after that incident at Gloria's house, and I know I'm not yours."

He jerked his head back. Talk about brutally honest. "I'm sorry about that. Call it newbie syndrome—too eager for my own good. I respect the office of sheriff and will do as I am told regardless of my opinion. Are we okay now?"

Her face turned a pretty shade of pink. "All is forgiven. But it's going to take a little while for me to trust you." She shrugged. "I'm human and trust doesn't come easy for me."

"I get that. Thanks for letting me know where we stand. Will not trusting me be a problem?"

She lowered her hand and revealed a devious grin. "Not for you. I promise to be professional, and I'm working on my trust issue."

He chuckled. "Well, for what it's worth, you're growing on me. Maybe I'll grow on you too."

"We'll see." She softened her words with a smile. "But, I'm willing to give this partnership one-hundred percent. We can start with introducing you around town. You work the day shift, right?"

He nodded.

"I'm pretty busy for the next couple of days. The library closes at four on Wednesdays. How about if we meet up there at six o'clock? I'll take you to my favorite diner. It's kind of a local hangout. You're sure to meet quite a few people."

"Sounds good. But aren't you afraid people will get the wrong idea and think we're on a date?"

She frowned. "You're right. What do you suggest?"

"I say we do it anyway and make up an excuse for being together if anyone asks."

"Like the truth?" She raised a brow. "I'm showing you around."

"That works." He'd wondered at the sheriff's insistence that Nancy work with him, but he was beginning to see the wisdom of having a local that everyone trusted on his side. "Out of curiosity, have you come up with any suspects?"

Her smile wavered. "No. This seems like something a teenager would do. I know a lot of young people in town and can't think of one that might pull a stunt like this. For the most part, the youth around here stay out of trouble. There've been a couple of pranks lately, but nothing serious."

"Like what?"

"Soap in the town fountain, colored soap used like graffiti on storefront windows. I thought that one was pretty clever. It washed right off, and the artwork was fun." She tapped her chin. "Oh, all the trash cans on one residential street were tipped upside down. Fortunately, it was the same day the garbage was picked up and most of the cans were still empty."

"We have a conscientious prankster?"

"Looks that way. I'd say this person is not our thief."

"Uncle Carter!" Gavin bounded down the stairs and pulled up short when he spotted Nancy. "Hey."

"Hi, yourself." Nancy waved.

Gavin turned to him. "A bunch of kids are meeting at the park. May I go?" His skateboard was tucked under his arm.

He was glad his nephew had made friends, and if what Nancy said was true, he had nothing to worry about. "Okay, but be home by dark."

Gavin moved toward the door. "Got it. 'Bye."

"Wear your helmet."

The door slammed. Too late. Gavin usually paid attention to safety, but maybe the move had him out of sorts.

"He must be a handful," Nancy said.

"Sometimes, but things seem to be going well for him. We've only been here a few days, and he's already made friends."

"That's important, especially at his age."

He studied the woman who was filled with contradictions and wondered how long this case would take to wrap up. First, they needed a solid lead.

"Oh, I almost forgot." She tapped keys on her laptop again. "The pickup with the stolen plate was parked in front of the pharmacy, which happens to have a security camera outside their building. I downloaded it and have been through it several times, but I'm afraid it's a dead end."

He stood and positioned himself behind the chair so he could see the screen over her shoulder. "Show me."

"It's queued to the right spot." She pressed play. The pickup sat front and center of the screen. Why would any thinking person steal a plate off a vehicle in view of a security camera? Unless they didn't notice they were being watched. Which would mean they were dealing with an amateur. A person wearing jeans and a black hoodie with the hood pulled over their head popped up from behind the truck.

"Can you pause it right there."

She clicked the mouse on the keyboard. "Why? His face is turned. You can't see a thing."

"We have his build and approximate height."

"How do you figure?" She glanced up at him.

"He appears to be standing at full height. Look at his legs. They aren't bent, and his torso isn't leaning forward."

"Agreed. But I still don't follow."

"We can see from the video that the truck has

standard tires. Now we know the height of the vehicle—a little over six-feet-high at the cab."

"Oh! That person is shorter than the cab."

"Exactly. He's on the other side of the truck so we can't see him well, but I'd guess he's about five-foot-seven or-eight. Looks like a lean build too." He rubbed his chin. "This could be a female. Will you press play again?" The thief ducked out of camera view and disappeared off the screen. Bummer. He was hoping to see the person's walk. He could tell a lot by the way he or she walked. "You're right. It's a dead end. Half the people in this town fit that description."

"Don't give up hope yet, Carter. We've only just begun. I suggest we plan a stakeout."

"When? Where? And why? The thefts are so random." He shook his head. "I don't think a stakeout is wise at this point."

Her brow puckered. "I'm not a fan of stakeouts, even though it seems prudent in this instance. But if you feel it's premature then I'll defer to you."

"Thank you." Sirens whined in the distance and grew louder.

Nancy stood, leaving the computer on the seat, and walked to the front window. "I wonder what happened."

"Beats me. I suppose you could call dispatch and find out."

"Ah. No. My mom made it clear that was not okay. Do you have a scanner?"

"I have an app on my smartphone. Hold on a second." He pulled it out, pressed the app, and turned up the volume.

"Someone get Carter over here," a voice said.

His stomach lurched. His gaze met Nancy's

surprised look.

"Come on. I'm driving." She grabbed her computer and shouldered her purse.

"But we don't know where they are."

"Didn't you hear the sound of kids playing in the background?"

She was out the door before he could even grab a jacket. He pocketed his keys and wallet, foregoing the jacket, then ran to her car. A second later she peeled out. He grabbed the sides of the seat and prayed they wouldn't require an ambulance before they discovered why his presence was needed.

"Do you always drive like this?"

"Only when it's important." She whipped around a corner then slammed on the brakes. An ambulance, sheriff's car, and a fire truck blocked the road in front of the park. He unclipped his seatbelt then sprinted to the scene. He spotted Lyle, who saw him at the same time and headed him off.

"What's wrong?" He couldn't see who the paramedics were working on.

"It's Gavin." Lyle placed a hand on his arm.

Carter's heart seemed to stop, and the world went into slow motion before he shook off the shock. "How bad? What happened?" He pushed past Lyle, who grasped his arm in a steel grip.

"Keep back and let them do their job. You know how this works."

Carter scrubbed his hand over his face. "Is he going to be okay?"

"I think so. According to witnesses, Gavin jetted into traffic on his skateboard and was struck by a vehicle. The driver called 911 and stayed with him until medical help arrived."

"How bad is he?" His gut wrenched.

"From what I've been able to gather it's not as bad as it looks. But he was unconscious for a minute or less."

"Okay." A soft touch on his arm made him look to his left. Nancy stood there. Concern flowed from her. He rested his hand over hers and gave it a gentle squeeze before moving forward to see his nephew.

Gavin's forehead was covered in gauze, and a splint secured his arm. "Hey, buddy. I heard you had a run-in with a car."

Gavin grimaced. "I'm fine."

Carter almost chuckled at the boy's ridiculous statement. He was anything but fine. However, considering what he'd prepared himself to see, Gavin looked okay.

The paramedic stood. "He probably needs stiches in his head, and his arm might be broken. X-rays will tell you more. He was lucky the car only nicked him and knocked him off balance. If he'd been hit full on we'd be having a different conversation. His pain level is moderate, but once the shock wears off he's going to hurt. He should go to the hospital to be treated."

"I'll take him. Thanks." Carter quickly filled out a little paperwork. With the medic's assistance, Gavin stood. He swayed slightly then righted himself.

"What's everyone looking at?" Gavin said between gritted teeth.

"The boy who rode his skateboard in front of a car and got hit." Now that Carter knew Gavin would be okay, his fear had turned to anger.

His nephew groaned. "I'm grounded, aren't I?"

"Oh, yeah. Come on." He guided Gavin to Nancy. "Think you could run us to the hospital to get patched up?"

"Sure." She strode ahead and pulled the door open. Her brow wrinkled. "Hold on a second." She rushed to the trunk.

A boy holding a skateboard held out his hand to Carter. "I'm Riley."

"Hi. You can call me Carter. Did you see what happened?"

Riley shook his head then moved toward Gavin. "You all right?"

"Yeah."

"Good. See you." He nodded to Carter, then plopped his board on the pavement and rolled away.

Someone wearing jeans and a black hoodie over his head bumped into Nancy, nearly knocking her over.

"Watch it," Carter warned the person who sprinted across the street and into the park. "You okay?"

She rubbed her right shoulder. "I'm fine. That guy sure was in a hurry." She popped the trunk then handed a utility blanket to Gavin. "Sit on this and wrap it around you."

He should have thought about Gavin's bloody shirt and considered that he might be in shock. "I'm sorry, I wasn't thinking. Lyle can give us a ride."

"I've got this, Carter. Relax." She shot him a look that said zip it.

He raised his hands. "Okay." Arguing with Nancy wouldn't do any good, so he slid into the front seat and buckled up. She might not be fond of him, but she was a good person. He'd owe her for this. "Hang on, buddy. This lady drives like she's on the racetrack."

"Cool." Gavin peered out the window. "My board is toast."

"Good," Carter said.

"What do you have against skateboarding?" Gavin snapped.

Nancy looked at him then Gavin. "You boys behave, or you're going to walk."

Carter pressed his lips together and stared forward. He had no doubt Nancy meant what she said. His mother sure had when he was a kid. She had pulled over in their neighborhood and booted him and his brother out the car door one block from home in the pouring rain. The experience shocked them into behaving while in the car from that day forward. All Mom had to do was point at the door, and they straightened out.

Nancy pulled up to the hospital entrance and rolled to a smooth stop.

"Thanks," Carter said. "I've got it from here."

"Keep the blanket. I have plenty. I could come in and wait with you. I don't mind."

"I appreciate the offer, but I have no idea how long this will take. I'll call you later and let you know what the doctor says."

"If you're sure."

"I am."

As Nancy drove away, he noticed her rear license plate was missing. He clenched his jaw. The thief had struck again.

# Chapter Four

AS NANCY SQUATTED ON HER FRONT porch, tying her tennis shoes, the cloudy sky grabbed her attention. One dark patch in particular made her nervous, but she wanted a power walk before meeting Carter for dinner. She hadn't seen him since Sunday when his nephew had been struck by a car. It wasn't every day someone was hit by a car in Tipton. People were still talking about it three days later. Poor Gavin. That kind of notoriety was the last thing he needed.

"Nancy, I'm glad I caught you. Do you have a minute?" Anna walked up and stopped at the bottom of her porch stairs with her adorable dog Freddy, who wore a rain jacket.

"I'm going for a power walk."

"Do you mind company? I'm dressed for it."

Sure enough, her neighbor wore sweatpants and a sweatshirt with athletic shoes. "I'm going to walk fast."

"Good. I need the exercise, and Freddy will love the quick pace."

Nancy trotted down the steps, trying not to show her dismay. Power walks were her thinking time, but it wasn't every day that Anna made a point to visit. "You ready?"

"I was born ready." Anna giggled. "Sorry. I've always wanted to say that."

Nancy shook her head, unable to wipe the grin from her face. "You are truly a nut. Let's get moving before that raincloud bursts."

Anna did a little hop and a skip to catch up but quickly found her rhythm. Nancy pumped her arms, wondering when Anna would share why she wanted to talk to her. Anna was a nice lady and a good neighbor, but she never intruded on Nancy's walks. Something had to be up.

"I heard about that new boy." Anna tsked. "Goes to show, even in a small town you need to look both ways before crossing the street."

"True. What are people saying about him?" Nancy glanced at her neighbor. Carter had left a message on her voicemail, stating, as they expected, his nephew had a broken arm and a mild concussion but was otherwise fine.

Anna's brow furrowed. "How'd you know people were talking about him?"

"I grew up in this town. People always talk." Even when they shouldn't. She'd been the topic of more than one gossip chain.

"Well, some wonder if he's trouble."

She'd had the same thought.

Freddy barked and pulled on his leash.

"Stop, Freddy," Anna said.

The dog obeyed, but something clearly had his attention.

Nancy gazed toward the hedge across the street where the dog's attention seemed to be focused. "You think he smells a cat?" Or maybe the license plate thief was lurking. She forced her breath to remain steady and resisted the urge to dart across the street to check the hedge to make sure it really was only an animal.

"Probably. Freddy isn't a cat lover." Anna rested a

hand on her side. "Do you mind if we slow down? I'm not in the shape you're in."

Nancy adjusted her stride. Slowing down might be a good idea. Her senses heightened, she listened for anything that didn't belong.

"Thanks. We should powerwalk together more often. I could use a walking partner. Especially with all that's been going on in town. It makes me feel safer."

"Is there more going on than a few missing license plates?"

"Not that I know of, but isn't that enough? Tipton has always been a safe place, but lately I don't feel very secure. What do you say? Can we exercise together?"

Nancy's stomach knotted. She liked Anna, but treasured this time alone. However, she didn't want Anna to be afraid to exercise outside. "Sure. Walking with a partner is a good idea. My mom will be happy. She's always telling me I shouldn't walk alone." Nancy would have felt guilty saying no anyway. It looked like she'd have to figure out a different method to stimulate her thoughts since her mind worked best without distractions.

"Great. Freddy and I will look forward to it."

Why was it she could never say no to Anna? Was it because they'd both been abandoned by men they'd loved—Anna by her fiancé and Nancy by her dad. Whatever the reason she'd do about anything for her neighbor.

"Nancy?"

"Hmm?"

"You never said if the rumors are true about the new kid who was hit by a car."

"I don't know of any rumors." She made it a rule to

never lie, but knew it probably sounded like a lie regardless, considering she usually had inside knowledge of most of the goings on in Tipton.

"That must be a first." She took a couple of quick breaths, clearly winded. "Rumor is the kid is messed up and into drugs."

"No way." She shook her head in disgust. "Where do people come up with this stuff?" She'd know if Gavin was using. He'd been in the library and had even talked to her briefly. She didn't smell anything on him or see any physical signs on his body or in his eyes when he'd walked past her at Carter's place either. Plus, she'd taken him to the hospital. Wouldn't she have known considering their close quarters? Perhaps not, but she still didn't believe he was on drugs. "Don't people have anything better to do than spread lies? How's he supposed to start fresh here if people won't let him?"

"He needs a fresh start?"

A quick glance at the darkening sky caused Nancy to turn and head back in the direction they'd come, knowing Anna would fall into step beside her without a prompt. "That's not what I meant. He's new to town, and thereby, the fresh start."

"Oh. I see. I'm glad I asked you about him, though, since I'd believed the worst."

"I hope that rumor doesn't stick. I'd hate to see the kid suffer because of a few busybodies."

"I'll make sure to set them straight."

Nancy stopped walking and placed her hands at her waist. "You'd do that?"

"Of course. I'm not interested in seeing anyone's life turned upside down because of a lie. No one deserves that. Even if he did ride his skateboard right in front of a car."

"You mean to tell me that's how this rumor got started. Someone thought he was high? Sweet juniper. That frosts me."

Anna chuckled. "You say the strangest things." She lowered her voice and leaned closer to Nancy. "See that guy? His name is Zander. He's pretty popular, and unfortunately, he basks in it. If you know what I mean." She nodded toward a teen. "He and Gavin got into a scuffle at school the other day. I'm afraid it wasn't a good start at the high school for Gavin either."

"Really? Why were they fighting?" Gavin didn't seem the type to get into a fight.

"It was a misunderstanding. Apparently, Zander thought Gavin was trying to break into his locker. As it turned out, Gavin was in the wrong hall."

Nancy shook her head. "Sounds like Zander's a hothead. I wonder why he thought someone would want to break into his locker in the first place."

"Good question, but he's really not a hothead. That's why this was so shocking and probably why I wondered about Gavin. This was the first incident involving Zander I've ever witnessed."

"Maybe he was having a rough day."

"Probably. I'll admit to having a challenging day myself on Monday."

"Why's that?"

She waved a hand. "It's nothing. Only a co-worker I can't figure out."

Nancy's interest piqued. "A man?"

"Yes. Why do you sound intrigued?"

"Is he single?" Nancy asked.

"He's a widower, and don't get any ideas. I see the

wheels churning. No, just no. Do you hear me?" She wagged a finger. "I'd never be interested in that man. Luke Harms is like an absentminded professor who's completely clueless when it comes to social graces or anything else for that matter." She shook her head. "No way! I'd rather be single for the rest of my life than—"

"I get it." Nancy held up her hands. "Sorry I mentioned it. I take it he's not your favorite person."

"Correct. I have his daughter in one of my classes, and I feel sorry for her." Anna shook her head.

"Because of her dad?"

"Yes and no. Mostly because she seems lost. It's really a sad story."

"Who are we talking about?"

"Maddie Harms."

*Duh.* She knew that. "I know her and her story. I'm sorry she's still having a rough time. She's a nice girl." With a lot of baggage. The poor kid had been swimming with her mother in the Willamette River when her mom got caught in an undertow and drowned. Maddie had been wearing a lifejacket, but her mom hadn't been. Nancy had reached out to the girl not long after her mother's death. She had become a regular at the library since. They'd talked some, but not as much as Maddie probably needed.

The sky had darkened even more. Thunder rumbled in the distance. Good thing she'd turned around when she had. Nancy picked up her pace. A droplet hit her face followed by several more. "I think we're about to get soaked."

Anna looked up. "Yep. Should we make a run for it?"

"I think so." They were only four houses away from

Nancy's. She charged forward right as the sky opened. Thunder rumbled closer this time. Her heart pounded.

Lightening snapped, and not long after, thunder crashed. How had the weather report missed this? Electrical storms set her on edge. Always had. She bounded up her driveway and stopped cold. "My license plate is missing!" When did that happen? Now more than ever she wanted to catch and stop this punk.

But first she needed to clean up and get ready to meet Carter.

Gavin eased onto the sofa. A scowl covered his face. "How long am I grounded?"

Carter crossed his arms. "No skateboarding until you heal." Frustration with his nephew still filled him a full seventy-two hours after Gavin's accident.

"But—"

"Your arm is broken, and you have a concussion. Not to mention a broken board. Case closed."

"Can I hang out at the park?"

"You're kidding. Have you looked outside?" Rain poured from the sky, creating pools of water. Thunder clapped, and their power had surged at least once since they'd gotten home. "No one will be at the park today. Plus, your cast is supposed to stay dry. I'm surprised you feel up to going out. Aren't you in pain?"

"Yeah, some, but I need to get out. This place is too small, and it's driving me crazy." Gavin's phone vibrated, indicating a text message. "Riley invited me to hang out at the bowling alley with him and some of the guys. Can I go?"

"You're grounded, remember?"

"More like under house arrest." His shoulders slumped. "This rots."

Unease filled Carter. He was supposed to meet Nancy for dinner soon. Gavin was in no condition either physically or mentally to be left alone. But what was he to do? It wasn't like they had a family friend he could count on to keep an eye on his nephew. The kid was nearly sixteen, and too old for a sitter. Maybe it would be better to give in this one time.

Carter could drop him at the bowling alley on his way to the library then swing by the place and check on him after. Would he be sending the wrong message? This parenting thing was hard. Maybe he should call Nancy and cancel. No, they'd gotten off to a rocky start already.

"Come on, Gavin, it's a school night. I'm sure you have homework."

"If I finish my homework before you leave, can I meet up with my friends?"

This was the perfect out. "That sounds like a fair deal. I want to see it when you're finished."

"For real?" A look of doubt covered Gavin's face.

"For real. You know my word is good."

"Yes!"

Carter grinned. "What do you have?"

"Some reading for English Lit and an Algebra problem. I did the rest in class. It shouldn't take long."

He glanced at his watch. "You have one hour. I suggest you get busy." Meanwhile he'd check his email. He pulled out his phone and opened the email app. A message from Nancy caught his eye. He tapped the screen and read it.

"Carter, my rear plate was appropriated. I'll file an

official police report but wanted to advise you. See you tonight."

He chuckled at her word choice. All those books she worked around must affect her vocabulary. It seemed Nancy wasn't as observant as he'd expected. He tapped out a reply. "It was gone Sunday when you dropped Gavin and me at the hospital. See you soon." He pressed send. A reply popped onto his screen.

"Why didn't you say something?"

"I was pre-occupied with my nephew who'd just been hit by a car." He pressed send.

At five forty-five, he found Gavin at the kitchen table inhaling a bowl of cereal. "I'm sure we could've found something better than cereal for dinner."

"This is fine." He shoveled another spoonful into his mouth.

"You finished your homework?"

"Yeah. It's on the couch."

"That was fast." Carter found the math and checked it. It looked like his nephew took after his dad who had always been good with numbers. He placed the homework back where he'd found it then headed for the kitchen table. "What about the reading you mentioned?"

"Done. I only had to read one chapter for the quiz tomorrow."

"You have a quiz on the reading?"

He nodded. "Miss Plum is a tough teacher, but she's all right."

High praise coming from his nephew. "Be ready to leave in five minutes. How will you get home? I can come get you if you'd like."

"Riley can bring me."

He didn't like the idea of some kid he didn't know

driving Gavin, but he didn't want to smother his nephew so stuffed away his concern. "Sounds like you have it all worked out. It's okay to call me if you start to feel too bad. I know you took a pain killer, but you still need to take it easy."

"Yeah. I will. I'm not going to bowl, only watch." Ten minutes later Carter dropped Gavin at the bowling alley. "If you need a ride home—"

"I won't."

With a sigh, he headed for the library. He didn't remember being this difficult growing up. Then again, his home life had been a lot different than Gavin's. They'd moved from one town to another frequently, but he was secure in his parents' love for him despite everything. His nephew hadn't been so fortunate. He parked then headed toward the library entrance.

No sign of Nancy. He'd thought she'd be waiting outside the door. Maybe she'd gone inside because of the rain. He pulled open the door. The small library was eerily quiet. "Nancy?" The tapping of heels filled the air, and relief washed over him. He turned and spotted her walking toward him.

"Hi. You're right on time."

"I try." How did she look so good after a full day working? Her jeans and red blouse still looked crisp. Maybe she'd changed. She had said the library closed early, so she'd more than likely gone home. "You ready to head out?"

She nodded. "How was work?"

"Quieter than I expected, and that's saying something."

She laughed as she locked the doors behind them. "I'm sure Tipton County will take a little getting used to.

The diner is close. Do you mind walking? It looks like the clouds have passed so we won't get drenched."

"Walking sounds nice." He strode beside her. "It feels good to stretch my legs."

"I agree. I try not to sit all day, but it seems I spend more time in a chair than standing." She chuckled. "Although I did manage to get in a power walk this afternoon and got soaked for my effort."

Ah, she *had* gone home. "You clean up nicely."

She grinned and bumped his shoulder with hers. "Are you flirting?"

"Maybe."

She laughed. "Be careful. We wouldn't want anyone to overhear and start up the rumor mill." A gust of wind shot Nancy's long hair into his face. "Whew. Sorry about that." She slowed, wrapped her hand around her hair, and tucked it beneath her jacket.

"No problem." A pleasant scent of flowers wafted from her hair—not too sweet, just right.

"Here we are. Daisy's Diner is the best. She makes everything fresh, and I've never had anything I didn't like."

"Good to know." He held the door open for her then followed her inside the eatery. The scent of roast beef and warm spices made his mouth water.

Nancy walked to the rear of the dining area and sat with her back to the kitchen leaving the spot facing the door open.

"Thanks for the primo seat."

She grinned. "I know how you cops are. My mom is the same way. The idea of not facing the door so she can see who is coming and going is such a big deal to her that she will leave an establishment if she can't get a seat facing the door."

He wasn't that extreme, but understood the woman's reasoning. He glanced around the diner decorated with vinyl albums on the wall and mini jukeboxes at each table. "Do you see anyone I should meet?"

She nodded. "Let's check out the menu and order, then I'll introduce you to Charlie and May. Charlie is the mayor, and May is his daughter."

"Is he married?"

"Widower. His daughter is a couple of years older than me. She works at the post office. Nice lady. Single—if you're looking."

His gaze slammed into Nancy's mirth-filled eyes. "I'm not."

"Good to know." Her cheeks tinged a light shade of pink.

The waitress walked over to their table. "Evening, Nancy."

"Hi, Kari. Have you met Carter Malone?"

Kari shot him a smile. "I haven't had the pleasure. I hear you work for the sheriff. Welcome to Tipton."

"Thanks." Good thing he didn't need to work undercover. It would be impossible in this town.

"Our specials tonight are roast beef with garlic mashed potatoes and steamed broccoli as well as grilled salmon with asparagus and a baked sweet potato."

"Mmm." Nancy placed the menu aside that had been sitting on the table when they'd arrived. "I'll have your roast beef special."

"Make that two."

"Anything to drink?"

"Water please." He had never acquired a taste for

soda.

"Same," Nancy said.

Kari gathered the menus then walked toward the kitchen.

"You ready?" Nancy stood.

"It's why I'm here." He followed her over to the mayor's table.

"Hi, Charlie." She nodded to the middle-age man then turned her attention to the petite blonde sitting across from her dad. "Hi, May. I'd like you both to meet Carter Malone."

Charlie stood and shook Carter's hand. "I've heard about you from Sheriff Daley. It's nice to put a face with the name. I'd invite you to join us, but we're about finished."

"No problem. It was nice to meet you." Carter had been half afraid the man would be smarmy based on his past experiences, but he didn't get that vibe. Instead he seemed like the genuine deal.

Nancy introduced him to several more people before returning to their table right as their meal arrived.

"Perfect timing." He sat and placed a napkin in his lap then bowed his head and offered a silent blessing for his food. He looked up the same time as Nancy. Their gazes locked for a moment, and his heart skittered. "Let's see if this roast beef is as good as the buildup." He dragged his attention to his plate and focused on his meal while trying to slow his pulse. Nancy was an attractive woman, but getting involved with her would be a bad idea for many reasons. He'd probably only responded that way because it had been a long time since he'd shared a meal with an attractive woman. Yes, that had to be it.

# Chapter Five

NANCY PEERED THROUGH THE LIBRARY WINDOW, watching the townspeople go about their day. Was the license plate pilferer lurking among them? Maybe if she stood here long enough she'd catch the thief in the act.

Her dinner with Carter last night had been a success from a getting-to-know-him standpoint. Several key people happened to be at the diner, as she knew they would be since she'd orchestrated the entire thing. It was really the only way for him to meet the town leaders without dragging him all over Tipton. Everyone had been happy to oblige her request. Best of all, Carter had been clueless to the setup and everyone else knew it wasn't a date. If they'd shown up there together, tongues would have wagged—she'd cut them all off at the pass so to speak, by planning ahead.

A flash of yellow grabbed her attention. Had someone darted around the delivery truck? It was probably the driver, but what if it wasn't? The library was empty, and no one looked to be headed this way. It would only take a minute to go outside and investigate. If Tara James, her assistant librarian, wasn't out of town taking care of her mother, Nancy wouldn't think twice about going outside. But leaving the library unattended was a no-no. Then again, she was in charge, and this was an emergency—well, sort of one at least.

She slipped into her jacket. Not bothering to lock up the library, she slunk down the stairs and stopped at the bronze statue of their town founders, Mr. and Mrs. Tipton. She stood behind Mr. Tipton and peered around him—no one. Had the person left while she'd snagged her coat? She sighed and turned.

"Hi."

A tiny scream escaped her lips before she could stop it. "Carter! You shouldn't sneak up on people."

"I didn't mean to. I saw you standing here as I was passing and thought I'd see what you were up to." He raised a brow.

She frowned. "Come inside." Good thing Carter wasn't the mayor. She'd have some explaining to do if he found she'd left the library unattended.

"What were you doing out there?" Carter held the door for her.

"Thanks. I thought I saw something and wanted to get a closer look."

"Something or someone?"

"Someone." She strode to her desk and sat.

Carter followed. "You think it was our guy?"

She shrugged. "It's hard to say. I only saw a flash of yellow before he disappeared behind a truck. Which reminds me, I need to have surveillance cameras installed on the exterior of the library."

"Isn't there red tape to get through?"

"Yes, but I could use my own money and request to be reimbursed."

His brow rose. "Kind of risky. What if your request is rejected?"

"Then when I move on from here I take them with me."

"Where're you going?"

She blew out a breath. "Nowhere. You ask a lot of

questions."

"Hazard of the job. Speaking of which, we never finished the conversation we started at my house."

"True. I open the library at nine. Maybe we can get together before that." They set up a meeting place and time then he left. Why had Mom put her on this case? There were so few clues to follow it felt like an impossible crime to solve, but she wasn't a quitter. One way or another she'd figure out a way to solve this mystery and stop that thief.

Carter strolled into his kitchen and poured a bowl of cold cereal. "Gavin, you up?" he called out into the quiet house.

His nephew ambled from the hall with a backpack slung over his shoulder. "Hey." He yawned.

"Hey, yourself. You ready for school?"

"Yep. Can we stop for a mocha on the way?"

"You're too young for coffee. It'll stunt your growth." Since when did Gavin drink coffee? He poured milk over his cereal.

Gavin frowned. "For real?"

He chuckled. "Beats me. Grandma used to tell your dad and me that when we were kids and begged for fancy coffee drinks." He looked down at the bowl of cereal then pushed it aside. "I'm sure once in a while won't do any harm. If we leave right now we can stop at the roadside coffee stand on the way."

"Really?" Gavin's face brightened. "Thanks."

Was that a smile? He didn't know his nephew could do that. "You have your lunch packed?"

"Yep." He breezed by Carter. "How's the new job?"

"Quiet." Except for a couple of home burglaries, but his nephew didn't need to know about those.

"Good." Gavin walked out the door.

He shook his head, following his nephew. The kid worried about him now more than ever since his dad was in prison for armed robbery. "Did you get all your homework done last night?"

"Yep."

"Good job." Carter got behind the wheel, buckled up then backed out of the driveway. "I heard something that surprised me." He'd debated saying anything, but if what he'd heard was true they needed to have a talk.

"What's that?" Gavin shifted to face him.

"There's a rumor that can't possibly be true since you were supposed to be home all last night." He noted the nervous look on Gavin's face. "Someone told me you had a date with a pretty blonde at BLB."

Gavin caught his breath. "The BLB?"

"Yeah. Biggest Little Burger. I'm sure you've heard of it. It's supposed to be where all the kids hang out."

His nephew's shoulders slumped. "How'd you find out?"

"We're not in L.A. anymore. You can't buy an apple without your neighbor knowing. Sneaking out in Tipton without me learning of it is going to be next to impossible."

"You mad at me?"

"For going on a date with a pretty girl? No. For sneaking out and breaking a house rule? I'm not happy."

"You would've said no 'cause it was a school night and I'm grounded."

Carter worked his jaw. "And knowing that, you still

chose to go? I'm disappointed. But more so, surprised you think that way, considering I allowed you to meet your buddies at the bowling alley. You know, in order for this to work we need to be honest with each other and communicate. Sneaking around isn't going to cut it. Understand? How am I supposed to trust you?"

"I don't know."

"See, now that's what I'm talking about. Honesty. You still want that mocha?" He'd cut Gavin some slack. All things considered, this was the first time his nephew had broken that house rule—at least that he knew.

"Yeah. Thanks, Uncle Carter. I know you're trying to fill in for my dad, and that you didn't ask to get stuck with me. I don't mean to cause you trouble."

"I appreciate that. And for the record, I don't feel *stuck* with you." He signaled and pulled into the parking lot with a drive through java. "What would you like?"

"A white mocha. A friend had one at school and let me taste it. It's super good. You should get one."

Carter ordered three.

"Don't you mean two?" Gavin shot him a questioning look.

"Actually, I'm meeting a friend, and thought I'd get her one too."

"Her?" Gavin raised a brow. "Is there something you want to tell me, Uncle Carter?" He grinned widely.

"No. But I'd like to hear about the blonde you were out with."

His smile fell. Clearly, he'd disappointed his nephew. "Her name is Maddie. She's in my English class, and she's nice. I saw her at the library when we first got to town and then ran into her in the neighborhood. She seems to have even fewer friends than I do."

He shot Gavin a look. "Seriously? Tell me more."

"There's not much more to tell. Her dad teaches senior English, and her mom is dead. She didn't say how."

He handed Gavin his drink, stuck the other two in cup holders then paid.

"Thanks."

"How'd the date come about?"

"It wasn't a real date. After school one day, we were talking. She offered to show me around town but said it had to be after her dad was asleep. I guess he's pretty strict."

Interesting. He tucked the information away for later. Maybe Nancy would be able to shed more light on that dynamic. Teenagers sneaking out at night troubled him. Especially since his nephew was now included in that mix.

"You know, just because you go to bed early doesn't mean everyone does. There were actually a lot of people there."

He held back a grin. "I see." Gavin's excuse for being at dinner with a girl made much more sense than what he'd imagined. To his knowledge, his nephew had never been on an official date. He turned into the school parking lot. "If you want to go out with this girl again, I want to know about it from you, not the paperboy."

"Okay. Sorry." Gavin swung the door open.

"At least let me stop first." Carter slammed on the brake. "You want a ride home?"

"I'll walk. Thanks!" He closed the door with his hip and sauntered off.

A boy across the parking lot called out to Gavin.

Carter narrowed his eyes, focusing on the other teen. Was that Riley, the kid Gavin had met up with at the bowling alley? It was hard to tell in the dim morning light at that distance. A horn honked behind him. He waved and pulled forward. He'd have to figure out Gavin's friend's identity later. A Chevy pickup truck whipped in front of him. The same one he'd seen their first night in town.

He followed it to a parking spot, pulled out his smart phone and waited to see who would get out. A teen boy hopped out. Carter took several pictures hoping they'd turn out since the kid had parked under a lit streetlight.

Maybe Nancy would recognize the boy. He pulled out of the parking lot and headed for a state park not far from town where he and Nancy were meeting to discuss their case. The cloak and dagger routine seemed a little much, but kind of cute too.

He'd enjoyed their dinner and found he was disappointed that most of the evening had been spent introducing him to the town leaders. At least they'd had some time alone while they were eating. Nancy had a way of processing information that intrigued him, and he looked forward to getting to know her better.

He yawned then took a long draw from the coffee cup—not bad. He increased his speed as he left the city limits. About a mile later, he signaled and pulled into the heavily wooded park. He wouldn't want to be here in a windstorm. Nancy's Mustang sat in the closest lot. He pulled up beside her and lowered his window.

She copied with her passenger window. "Good morning. You want to take a drive with me?"

"How about a walk instead?"

"Okay."

He raised the window, grabbed the drinks, then got out and waited by the hood of her car.

Nancy sidled up to him. She smelled fresh, like a bar of soap. Her jeans fit just right, and she had on the same knee-high boots she'd worn to his place the other day, along with another soft looking sweater—this one was purple. In a word, she looked and smelled refreshing.

She cleared her throat as she turned toward a bark-covered path. "Do you always drink two coffees?"

"Oh yeah." He thrust the second drink toward her. His face heated. "Gavin and I got white mochas today. I picked up one for you too."

Her face lit. "Thanks. That was really nice." She took the cup and sipped. "Mmm. It's good. So I talked to my mom about the case and told her we don't have anything to report."

He'd told the sheriff the same. "Before we get to that, do you recognize this kid?" He pulled up the photo and handed his phone to her. "I took several. Just scroll through."

"I'm sorry, no. The pictures are too dark to see his face clearly. Is he relevant to our case?"

Carter pocketed his phone. "Not that I know of. But he's an unsafe driver, and I'd like to follow up with his parents." He told her about that first night in town.

"That wasn't a friendly welcome. On behalf of the citizens of Tipton, I apologize for this boy's poor driving skills."

He chuckled. "No need. Teens like to drive fast—it's no reflection on the town. I'm looking forward to when my nephew gets his license. I should probably let him drive more, but…"

"You don't want him behind the wheel of your Dart?"

His face heated. "Guilty."

"Don't feel bad. I'd be the same way with my Mustang. Maybe you could get him a used car."

"I've thought about it." He sighed. "Sorry for getting off topic. Do you have anything new to report?"

"I wish." She frowned. "I don't like this case. We have nothing to work with."

He chuckled as he strode beside her. "Sure we do. The guy is on surveillance video, so we know his approximate size and build."

"That's true, but it's not enough."

He agreed. "I looked through the reports on record and noted our perp doesn't leave any evidence behind. Not even gum wrappers or cigarette butts. Then again, most people can't be certain when their plate was stolen. Only that it went missing after they'd been parked downtown, therefore determining the exact crime scene is impossible."

"Good point. I keep asking myself why someone would steal license plates. What do they do with them?"

"We usually find them on stolen vehicles."

"Figures. Honestly, I think the only way we'll catch this guy is to install more surveillance cameras downtown and keep our eyes open. One of the cameras is bound to catch his face. Once we have that, then we'll get him."

Her brown eyes drew him in. A sense of familiarity washed over him. Odd. He pulled his gaze away and blew out a breath. "I agree. How are you doing on the ones for the library?"

"They were installed early this morning before anyone was out and about to notice."

"How did you have that done so fast?"

"A friend owed me a favor. He already had the equipment, so it was only a matter of installing it."

He admired her resourcefulness. "Okay then. I'll talk to a few businesses about installing surveillance cameras. The more eyes we have on the street, the better chance we have of catching this guy. He's bound to show his face sooner or later."

"Agreed. But don't you think I should talk to the business owners?" She shot him a questioning look then quickly added, "With you being new and all."

"I suppose. But wasn't that the point of our dinner?" He'd met several business owners that night. It struck him as odd that so many ate at that diner on the same night and time. He suspected Nancy had something to do with that, especially considering no one mistook their dinner out as a date, like they had his nephew's non-date with Maddie.

He had to hand it to Nancy; she knew how to navigate Tipton, which hopefully would help with this case. It wasn't the kind of crime he usually investigated, and even though he resisted at first, he was happy to have the help. "I'm sure we'll run into each other sooner or later, but if you discover anything or catch the guy in the act you'll wait for help and not engage right?

She nodded. "I know the rules."

"Good." Even though she said the words, he had a suspicion that in the heat of the moment she might act before notifying the authorities. He prayed he was wrong.

Ten minutes after leaving Carter at the park, Nancy pushed into Roaster's Coffeehouse. The rich smell of coffee washed over her. This place was a little piece of heaven on earth with its warm color tones and stone fireplace. She didn't have the heart to tell Carter she was meeting a friend for coffee right after their meeting, or that she didn't usually drink sweet coffee beverages, so she drank the white mocha anyway. It was such a thoughtful gesture, and very unexpected. Now she had little appetite, but this was a ritual she couldn't skip, or everyone would know something was up. She waved to the regulars on her way to the counter to order a large black coffee and a chocolate dipped donut. She only indulged on Fridays and looked forward to this occasion all week.

"Good morning, Nancy." Pepper White, a longtime friend and the owner of the shop, smiled from behind the register. "You want your regular?"

"Unquestionably." She pulled a five from her wallet.

Pepper chuckled. "I will never get used to the way you talk. I'll bring your order out to you."

Nancy grinned. "Thanks." She had no idea why her friend always said that when Nancy knew that Pepper would bring the drink and donut then stay and visit. Nancy wove through round tables of varying sizes until she reached her usual spot by the window.

Her friend's comment about her word choice lingered in her mind. She didn't mean to use odd words. They popped out without thought. She blamed her vocabulary on the books she read at the library. Most of the time she kept busy, but in the downtime she always grabbed a book from the shelf to devour.

The door to the shop opened and Gloria strolled inside. She waved to Nancy. After placing her order Gloria came over to Nancy's table. "Mind if I join you until my drink is ready?"

"Not at all. How have you been? We haven't talked since your daughter's party."

"Not bad. I can't thank you enough for rescuing me. I still feel horrible that you were arrested. I never dreamed that would happen."

"That makes two of us."

Gloria glanced toward the pickup counter. "Looks like my drink is ready. We need to get together soon. Take care, my friend." She stood and breezed away.

Nancy grinned as Pepper slid two plates topped with donuts onto the table then returned with their drinks. She sank onto the seat across from Nancy. "What did Gloria want?"

"Nothing."

Pepper raised a brow as she took a sip from her cup. "You have no idea how I look forward to this time every week. How've you been? I heard the new deputy arrested you. Is that why she was talking to you?"

Nancy held up her hand. "No talking until I get my donut fix." She took a bite then washed it down with her coffee. Little appetite or not, this was too good to pass up. "Girl, you seriously make good coffee."

Pepper grinned. "Thanks, sweetie. Now will you fill in all the blanks? All I know are rumors."

Nancy knew her friend had been sitting on her questions for a week. She wouldn't keep her waiting any longer. "I've been fine, and you heard correctly about the new deputy. Gloria asked me to break the window on her back door to rescue her daughter's birthday cupcakes—he caught me and thought I was a thief."

"Then the rumors are true. Gloria is a lot of things, but frugal is not one of them." Pepper kept her voice low.

Nancy laughed. "Maybe not, but you know she's very generous with what the Lord has given her."

"That's the truth. Tell me more."

"You know you could've called or stopped by my place. We don't have to limit our time to Friday morning coffee, or tea, in your case." She took another bite of the donut followed by coffee.

"And spoil our weekly ritual? Not a chance. Tell me about the deputy. I heard he's cute."

Nancy paused. "I suppose he is." She didn't want to admit she'd noticed. His dark hair, five o'clock shadow, and blue eyes were the perfect mix of rugged and cute. Based on his gift of coffee this morning it seemed he might be as sweet on the inside as he was on the outside. "How has your week been?"

"Oh, you know. Nothing new here." Her eyes widened. "Except there has been a rash of license plate thefts."

Nancy picked up her coffee. "I heard about that. Has anyone seen anything out of the ordinary?"

"Not that I know of. I've thought about it a lot, and the only thing that's happened out of the norm is the new deputy and his son."

"Nephew."

"Oh. Thanks. I hadn't heard that part. I figured the deputy was divorced since no one said anything about a woman being with him."

Nancy shrugged. She had no idea if he was

divorced. But now she wanted to know if Carter had ever been married. "Have you considered installing a surveillance camera outside your shop?" Even though Carter was supposed to talk to the business owners, Pepper was a friend, so she didn't count.

Pepper's brow scrunched. "Now why would I do that?"

"For added security."

"In case you've forgotten, this is Tipton. Nothing ever happens here."

Nancy ran her finger around the rim of her cup. "I wouldn't say nothing, considering the rash of car plate thefts."

Pepper's lips formed an O. "Maybe I should look into a camera after all. One can never be too careful."

Nancy nodded as she wiped her fingers on a paper napkin. "I need to open the library. Have a great weekend, my friend." She stood and left. Would Pepper follow her suggestion? The woman had a mind of her own, so it was impossible to know for sure.

# Chapter Six

"WHAT IS GOING ON?" NANCY MUMBLED, picking up her pace on the sidewalk. Why was there a crowd gathered outside the library? Nancy rushed toward the group then stopped abruptly and stared at what had grabbed their attention. Okay, it wasn't a huge deal, but in their small town, something like bronze statues suddenly decked out in pioneer clothing was about as exciting as it got on a weekday. "Good morning, everyone."

All eyes shifted to her. Several voices spoke at once. "Did you do this?"

"No, but I wish I'd thought of it." She pulled out her smart phone and clicked off a few pictures of the statues and then a couple more of the crowd gathered around it. She'd upload them to Instagram and the library's website today. "I'll have the doors open in a moment if anyone wants to come inside."

She strolled up the stairs, unlocked the doors, and went in. The motion-sensor lights flickered on as she strolled to her desk. A few people followed her and soon made their way to the stacks.

Nancy went about her morning ritual of clicking on computers, then rolling the cart of returned books over to her desk to be checked in. Normally she enjoyed the tasks, but today her mind wandered to the display outside. Too bad her assistant wasn't back so she could investigate. The new security cameras had been installed two days ago, and she couldn't help wondering if the prankster had been caught on video. As soon as she had a break she'd check.

Lilly, the real estate agent she'd referred Carter to, walked up to the desk with a cookbook. "Will you be getting any new gluten-free cookbooks soon? This is the only one I could find."

"There aren't any on order, but if you'd like to request one I can see about getting it in for you."

Lilly's eyes widened. "Thanks. I'll do that. For now though, I'll give this one a try. I recently found out I'm gluten intolerant, and I'm sick of the food I've been making."

"I'll do a little research too and see what I can find. In the meantime, maybe check online for recipes."

"I prefer holding an actual book. How have you been? It seems like forever since we had a nice long visit."

It had been forever—like never, but she wasn't opposed to it. They'd known one another since elementary school but had never been close. "I'm fine. How about you?" Lilly was one of the popular girls in high school, married young, divorced young, no kids, and she had a good career as a real estate agent. Nancy, on the other hand, had not been popular. She loved her books and the places they took her, so it'd never really bothered her that she wasn't popular. In spite of their social differences, Lilly had always been cordial.

"Oh, you know...busy. But I'm trying to take more time to focus on the important stuff."

Nancy studied the trim brunette. "What do you mean?"

"Renewing old friendships, focusing on my mental and physical wellbeing—that kind of thing."

"What brought on the change?"

"To be honest, burnout. After my divorce and then getting my real-estate license and pushing so hard to succeed, I hit a wall."

"I had no idea. I'm glad you're doing better."

"Thanks, and thanks for sending Carter my way. He got the house in case you didn't hear."

"You're welcome. I'm glad it worked out for both of you." Nancy nodded to another woman who walked up behind Lilly.

"It was great to talk with you. Maybe we can grab coffee or whatever sometime."

"I'd like that." The day had barely begun and had already been filled with one surprise after another. What would be next?

By mid-afternoon Nancy found the time to upload her pictures of the statues to Instagram then sent the link to the local newspaper. Who knows, maybe they'd think the prank was newsworthy. It was odd that little pranks had started happening around the same time as the license plates began disappearing. Someone had put soap in the town fountain, then last week and two nights ago an entire cul-de-sac had been TP'd. Were they related, or was it a coincidence?

She pulled out the steno pad she wrote her thoughts on when working a case and penciled in her questions.

"Afternoon, Nancy."

She pulled herself from her thoughts and focused on the young man standing at the checkout desk with a book in his hand. He looked familiar. "Do we know each other?"

"I don't think so." He shook his head and offered a

smooth smile. The girls at his school probably fell for his charm, but not her.

"You called me by name."

"The nameplate says 'Nancy Daley'."

*Of course.* "Right. I guess I'm used to young people calling me Miss Daley when they don't know me."

"Oops. Sorry, Miss Daley." He emphasized the Miss part.

Giggles emanated from the stacks. She looked that direction. "Friends of yours?"

"Naw. You know freshmen. They're a little odd sometimes."

She chuckled. This kid was a piece of work. She motioned to the book he held. "Do you have a library card?"

"I didn't know I needed one."

*Seriously?* She pulled out the application form. "It will only take you a few minutes to fill this out. Once you do, I'll make your card."

He frowned and quickly went to work. "Here you go."

She plugged his information into the computer noting his name was Zander. Now she knew why he looked familiar. Anna had pointed him out on their walk and stated he was popular—apparently not for his common sense. How could he not know he needed a library card? She scanned the book. "Twentieth century history, huh?"

"Yeah. I need the extra credit. The school library stinks. Plus, I heard about the statues and wanted to see them for myself."

She'd heard the same about the school library from many students. "Hopefully the public library will meet your reading needs. I'm surprised this is the first time you've needed to check out a book." She handed him his library card.

His face tinged red. "I'm not much of a reader."

She slipped the receipt into the front cover. "The book is due in three weeks. There's a late fee of twenty cents a day after that."

"Okay." He tucked the book into his backpack and left.

She rose and ambled toward the giggly girls. "Is there something I can help you find?"

They each held up a book. "No thanks. Zander is hot. He's the most popular boy in school."

She nodded politely then returned to her desk. She didn't care to get into a discussion on the attributes of the most popular boy in school.

The rest of the day dragged until it was finally closing time. She tucked her steno pad into her bag and headed out. The statues still wore costumes. Was it up to her to remove them, or would someone with the city take care of it? No one had done so yet, it looked like it was probably her job. She almost hated to remove them, but rain was in the forecast tonight, and they would be a soggy mess in the morning. She started on Mrs. Tipton.

"Is this how you spend your free time when you're not taking walks in the park? You know, defacing public property is a crime."

She looked over her shoulder and grinned. "Hi, Carter. Want to help?"

"Why not?" He took care of Mr. Tipton. "What are you going to do with the clothes? They're in decent shape for being old."

"I wonder if the person who did this might want them back. I don't think they're as old as they look. I went to the musical at the high school last year, and this looks a lot like something the cast would have worn. I wonder if that's where they came from. Maybe I should ask Anna if anything is missing."

"You mean you don't know who dressed the statues? I thought your surveillance cameras might've clued you in."

"Can you believe I forgot to look?" What was wrong with her?

He chuckled. "No, I can't. You feeling okay?" He offered a teasing grin.

"I'm fine. I'll give Anna a call later, but for now I guess I'll put these clothes in a box and set them outside the door in case our prankster returns. Let's go inside and check last night's surveillance, if you have time?" She held her breath. A part of her wanted him to agree and another part wanted him to decline. The idea of him in close proximity as they looked over the footage shot unease through her. Why?

"Sure, but it'll have to be fast. I don't want to leave Gavin alone much longer."

"Are you afraid he'll take off again?" She gathered the clothes into a bundle and walked up the stairs toward the library entrance. She couldn't help but wonder about the teen. He seemed like a good kid, but he also had an edge to him, which in her mind made him unpredictable. Not necessarily a bad quality, but in a teenager, it could be dangerous.

He gave her a sideways glance, seeming to size her up. What was that about? "Gavin snuck out the other night to be with a girl."

She raised a brow. "Really? Who?" She set the clothes beside the door then unlocked it and went inside.

"Do you know Maddie Harms?"

"Yes. She's nice girl. A bit of a loner. But you don't need to worry about your nephew hanging out with her." She wasn't one for gossip. Should she give him the girl's history, or let him make his own judgments on her character?

"What aren't you saying, Nancy?"

"What makes you think that?"

"I'm a detective. I read people, and your body language says you're hiding something."

She booted up the computer to access the surveillance archives. "You're good. But I don't want to gossip."

"Do I need to know?"

She blew out a breath. "If you keep digging into Maddie, you're bound to learn that her mom was killed in a drowning accident. Maddie was there, and I believe she blames herself. Her mom wasn't wearing a life vest. Everyone around here knows the undertow in the Willamette River is unmerciful, even to strong swimmers."

Carter frowned. "That's sad."

"I agree. The girl pretty much closed herself off from everyone after the accident. Gavin is probably good for her. Maybe she'll be able to move past the accident and start to live a normal life again." She pressed her lips together—she'd said more than necessary. With a few clicks, she had the surveillance footage from last night playing on the screen. She forwarded it until she spotted moving images. "Look." Her stomach sank.

Carter hovered over her shoulder. "You've got to be kidding me! That's Gavin, but who's the girl?"

"Maddie."

"You still think my nephew hanging out with her is a good idea?" Frustration tinged his voice.

"It's an innocent prank. No one was hurt, and the townspeople enjoyed it. I even thought it was cute."

"What happens when she decides to take her pranks to the next level?" He stood to his full height and crossed his arms.

"You're assuming she's the instigator." She had a very difficult time believing this was all Maddie's doing.

His brow furrow deepened. "Let's connect later. I need to get home."

With a sigh, Nancy watched Carter leave the building. She could access the archives remotely and would view the rest at home. For the first time ever, she didn't want to be alone in the library.

"I'm home," Carter called out as he strode into his bungalow. He still couldn't believe his nephew had been involved in the prank with the statues outside the library. How many times had he snuck out? Carter would never be able to sleep at this rate. He took the stairs two at a time. "Gavin?" He knocked on his nephew's bedroom door before opening it.

Gavin sat on his bed, leaning against the headboard. He looked up from the book he held. "Hey. I didn't hear you come in."

"Good book?"

"Yeah. It's a mystery. My English teacher asked Maddie and me to co-lead an after-school book club."

Carter ambled over to the desk chair and sat facing Gavin. "Why did she ask the two of you?"

"I guess she saw talent in us." He shrugged. "She said something about the way we did our homework."

He didn't know his nephew had any special way with words or leadership skills, but he knew the kid was smart. "Congratulations. I'm proud of you for that. Now we need to talk about another matter."

A shadow of doubt flickered in Gavin's eyes. "O-kay," he drew out the word. "What did I do?"

He had to hand it to the kid for playing dumb. Assuming Gavin had snuck out numerous times, his nephew might incriminate himself for something Carter didn't know about. "How about you tell me?"

He rested his ankle on his knee and leaned back— let the kid sweat. Tough love wasn't easy, but he'd had plenty of experience with his brother.

Gavin opened and closed his mouth before pressing his lips together.

An expert interrogator, Carter waited, knowing his nephew wouldn't be able to stand the silence for long.

"Fine. I helped a friend dress the statues at the library. It was no big deal. Why make a scene about it?"

His nephew had no idea what making a scene was if he thought this was one. "The statues aren't the problem. You sneaking out again is. How am I supposed to get a good night's sleep if I have to keep an ear open for you coming and going? You've always been a good kid, Gavin. Don't ruin it now."

"I'm not going to ruin anything. If I promise to not sneak out again will that make you happy?"

"Yes, but only if you intend to keep that promise. Don't give me lip service. We need to be able to trust one another. You know how I feel about lying."

Gavin ducked his chin. "Yeah. I'm sorry. I really like this girl and she—"

"Are we talking about Maddie?"

He nodded. "She's not like other girls. She's real and doesn't judge me for having a dad in prison."

"You told her?" He couldn't have been more surprised if Gavin had told him he'd seen a frog turn into a prince.

"Yes."

Maybe Nancy was right about the two of them. Perhaps they'd be able to help each other through their pasts. "I'll make a deal with you. I won't stop you from seeing this girl, but the next time she wants to get together, tell her it has to be before nine. You're both welcome to hang out here when I'm home, or I can give you a lift someplace."

"I don't know." Gavin looked torn.

"Considering you're already grounded, you should be happy I'm allowing you to have a friend over. It's up to you, but know this: I can install an alarm that will go off if you open a door or window, or we can trust each other. Your choice. Take it or leave it."

Gavin glared at him. "Fine."

"Good." He stood. "I'm making chicken stir-fry for dinner." And first thing tomorrow he was going to follow through with the security system, but he'd keep that to himself. He could have it rigged to send the alarm to his phone rather than go off in the house. He wanted to trust his nephew, but life had taught him that putting precautions in place for those just-in-case times was important, and if it turned out he'd overreacted, Gavin would be none the wiser.

# Chapter Seven

NANCY LOOKED UP FROM THE CHECK-out desk at the library when she heard the door open. Just the girl she wanted to talk to. She stood. "Hi, Maddie."

The girl stopped, an uncertain look covering her face. "Hi, Miss Daley." She held up a book. "This was good. Thanks for recommending it." She slid it into the return slot.

"How is the book club going?"

"We meet tomorrow for the first time. I'm not sure how many people signed up, but I hope there's more there than Gavin and me."

Here was her opening. She opened her mouth to confront the girl about the statues then snapped it shut. No harm was done, and it *was* pretty funny. It wasn't like Maddie was a troublemaker.

"Were you going to say something?" Maddie asked.

"Only that even if you and Gavin are the only ones there for the first meeting, I'm sure you'll manage to have a lively discussion. Have you come up with any questions yet?"

She shook her head. "I didn't think about questions. What should I ask?"

Nancy spent the next ten minutes coaching the teen with ideas.

"Wow. Maybe you should lead a book club. You could hold it here. Since you like mysteries it could be called The Mystery Caper Readers."

Nancy grinned. "I'll give that some thought." It might actually be fun, but did she really have the time? Sure, when she wasn't consulting for the sheriff's department she did, but leading a group was a commitment she couldn't set aside when it was inconvenient. "Do you mind answering a weird question?"

"I guess not." A look of unease rested on Maddie's face.

"I'm aware that you've been hanging out with Gavin Malone in the evening."

The teen's face reddened.

"I was wondering if you've ever seen anything odd when you were out."

She let out a breath as if she'd been holding it. "Oh. Well...I don't think so. Tipton is pretty quiet at night."

"I've heard. I'm not much of a night owl."

"There's hardly anything to do around here at night. You're not missing much. The only places open after ten are the bowling alley, BLB, and that bar on the edge of town—which I've never been in," she quickly added.

That she went to Best Little Burgers wasn't a surprise since it was the local hangout for teens and adults alike in the evenings. "I didn't expect that you would have frequented the bar, considering you're underage." Though Tipton was a quiet town, the bar had a reputation for trouble. The deputies had responded to calls at that location quite a few times. Did the thief hang out at the bar? She cringed at the idea of going there to poke around. Maybe she'd mention it to Carter and let him ask around. If she showed up there everyone would know she was up to something, and her secret pastime as a consultant would be out in the open and cripple her ability to sleuth in secret.

Maddie nodded. "Is that all you wanted to ask me?"

"Yes. Thanks."

"Miss Daley?"

"Hmm?"

"Why did you ask me that? Should I be afraid to go out at night?"

"Being out alone at night is never a good idea, Maddie, especially if your dad doesn't know."

Maddie looked down. "My dad would keep me under lock and key if he could. Which would be fine if he'd give me the time of day. But ever since Mom..."

Nancy's heart hurt for this girl. "It's difficult to lose a parent for any reason. I know from experience."

"But you didn't lose both your parents like I did." She turned and rushed out.

Nancy closed her mouth. That poor girl. Maddie was correct—Nancy had a great mom who, even though she had a career, had always made time to be a mom. Somehow Nancy had to help this girl. Maybe Anna Plum would have some ideas. After all, she was Maddie's English teacher. She'd be sure to bring up the teen tonight on their power walk.

Carter ground his back teeth as he sat in a frightened homeowner's living room. Tipton County was not the quiet hub of low crime he'd thought. He looked down at his notes. "Other than your missing hunting rifle, an emerald ring, two hundred in cash, and your new television, is anything else missing?" He looked up and met the angry gaze of Mr. Owens, the homeowner.

"Not that I can tell. I don't understand why they

stole our TV. It wasn't even a big one. Only a small one my wife had in the kitchen. She likes to watch the food network while she cooks."

"That's a valid question, but I have no idea. We'll do our best to recover your items."

"I won't hold my breath. I know how these things go."

Carter didn't argue. The man was correct. The chances of finding his stolen goods were slim. He stood. "I have everything I need."

Mr. Owens walked him to the door. "Thanks for getting here so fast."

"I was nearby when the call came in. Take care, Mr. Owens." The man's wife was too upset to talk and had retreated to a spare bedroom. Carter strode to his cruiser and after one last perusal of the property, headed for town. His shift was about over, and he needed to write a report.

Carter had taken pictures and dusted for prints. What bothered him the most was how clean everything was. Whoever had broken in knew where to go and didn't waste time rummaging through drawers.

Back at his desk in the bullpen, Carter typed out his report on the desktop. He could have worked via the computer in the cruiser, but he tried to avoid it whenever possible. It seemed to him if his focus was on the computer while sitting in his cruiser, he was more vulnerable to an attack. He had the daylights scared out of him once back in L.A. when someone knocked on his window. He'd done his best to remain vigilant ever since.

Footsteps approached his desk. He looked up. "Hey, Lyle. How's it going?"

"Be better when we figure out what's going on in

this county." Lyle pulled a chair beside Carter's desk and rested an ankle on his knee. "I talked to a buddy in Marion County, and he suggested the license plates and thefts are drug related."

"I'd buy that. Seems most crime can be tracked back to drugs. What do you suggest?"

"I'm not sure. We don't have the budget to hire someone dedicated to vice, and it's not my strong area."

"It's not my area of expertise either, but I've had a little experience thanks to my brother."

Lyle's brow rose. "Sounds like there's a story there."

"Maybe another time. I need to finish this report then meet Nancy at my place. Now that we think this could be drug related, I'm not sure having a civilian involved is wise."

"Nancy knows how to take care of herself." Lyle stood and put the chair back. "I wouldn't write her off yet." He winked then strode down the hall.

Carter frowned. It didn't set well that drug trafficking could be behind the sudden uptick in crime. And it especially didn't set well that Nancy could be in harm's way if she tipped off the wrong person while she investigated the missing license plates.

He finished the report, ordered an extra-large cheese pizza, then headed out. Nancy would be at his place soon, and he wouldn't have time to fix dinner and eat. If it were only him he wouldn't bother, but Gavin needed stability, and meals together were a part of that.

Thirty minutes later, he pulled into his driveway and noted Nancy's Mustang parked along the curb. He grabbed the pizza then headed for the front door. Nancy met him there. "I hope you like cheese pizza."

"Love it, but you didn't have to feed me."

"It's for Gavin, but there's enough for all of us."

A knowing look filled her eyes. "I'm intruding on family time. How about if I take a walk and come back in a half-hour."

"Thanks, but it's good for us to have company. He can practice table manners." Carter pushed inside, grinning at the shocked expression covering Nancy's face. "Dinner," he called out into the quiet house. "I bought a pizza."

Gavin zoomed down the stairs. "Oh, hi, Nancy."

"You're looking well, Gavin. How's the arm?"

"I can't wait for the cast to come off." He turned to Carter. "You got cheese?"

"As promised."

"Yes!" He washed his sling-free hand then sat at the small dining table. "I'm starved."

Carter offered a blessing for the food, and the word amen had barely come out of his mouth when Gavin reached for a slice. "Dude, chill. We have a guest."

Gavin frowned. "Sorry." His pace slowed. "What's the deal with you and Nancy?"

Her eyes sparkled as she pressed her lips together.

Carter cleared his throat. What should he say?

"I'm giving him inside information about the town and the residents. My mom's the sheriff, and she thought since your uncle is new in town, it might help him do his job better."

"Cool." Gavin took a hearty bite and chewed.

Why hadn't Gavin questioned Nancy's presence the last time she was here? Now that she thought about it, he'd been in a hurry to go out with his friends, and then he'd been hit by a car.

"Maddie took me around town too."

"Oh yeah?" Nancy asked between bites. "Where did she take you?"

"We walked downtown. She told me about the different shops. The best places to eat and that the town is really old fashioned. Is it true the only places open late are the BLB and the bowling alley?" He directed his question to Nancy.

"Pretty much. I'm not sure why Tipton hasn't kept up with the times." She shrugged. "I like it though. Makes life simpler."

"I guess. But there's not a lot to do here."

"Not true. For starters, you have your book club with Maddie, and around the holidays we hold a tree lighting ceremony in the park where everyone sings Christmas carols. There's hot chocolate and cookies, and sometimes the band from the high school puts a few songs together."

Gavin rolled his eyes.

Carter shot him a warning look. At least his nephew wasn't acting out like he had been earlier. One minute he treated Carter with disdain, and the next he was fine. How did parents manage?

After scarfing down two more pieces, Gavin asked to be excused then disappeared upstairs presumably into his bedroom. Together, Carter and Nancy cleared the table then headed outside to the covered front porch. He didn't want Gavin to overhear their conversation.

Nancy shrugged into her jacket and settled onto the porch swing. He sat beside her since there was no place else to sit.

Nancy breathed in deeply then let her breath out slowly. "I love the scent of fall."

"Is that what I smell?" He grinned.

She shook her head. "Coming from L.A., I suppose you aren't accustomed to seasons."

"We have seasons, but they aren't as defined as here." He lowered his voice. "Lyle informed me there's been an uptick of drug activity in Marion County and suggested that could be behind what's going on here."

"Oh no. But he doesn't know for sure?"

"No. Considering the unpredictability of that culture, I think it'd be best if you took a step back."

She shifted to better face him. "I don't know how much further back I can get and still be a part. Everyone I've talked to is as baffled as we are. Maybe you should let the principals at the middle school and high school know what's going on, so they can keep their eyes and ears open."

"Agreed. But—"

"I'm having coffee with your real estate agent tomorrow before work. She shows homes all over the county. Maybe she's caught a whiff of something."

*Doubtful.* "I suppose it wouldn't hurt to give her a heads up." He'd hate for a single woman to be caught unawares as she entered a house that should be vacant, only to walk in on a drug dealing operation.

"My neighbor, Anna Plum, teaches English at the high school. I should tell her too."

With all the people she wanted to fill in, he worried whoever was responsible for the crimes might hear and change their MO. "Miss Plum is Gavin's English teacher."

"I heard she's a great teacher. All her students think the world of her, and in my opinion, that says a lot. English isn't exactly PE. You know what I mean?"

He nodded. "Fine, but don't tell anyone else. We don't want to tip our hand."

"What hand? We have nothing other than the drug angle. Not exactly a solid lead." She frowned. "There's something about this case that bothers me."

"What's that?"

"I'm not sure. Normally when I help the police I can ask questions and follow up on clues. Of course I'm careful how I do it, so no one suspects my motive, but this time that approach isn't working."

His stomach roiled. "You've specifically questioned people about the case?"

"Sort of. It was more indirectly, and I've only talked with a few business owners, but they didn't tell me anything I didn't already know."

He set his jaw. His gut told him Nancy was in over her head. If only the people in this town would see the danger of involving a civilian.

# Chapter Eight

NANCY SAT ACROSS FROM LILLY AT ROASTER'S Coffee. "How are home sales going?"

"I keep busy."

"Good."

"How are things at the library?"

"I stay busy too." This was awkward. She'd hoped her question would break the ice and cause Lilly to reveal the reason she'd asked her to coffee. The woman had stated she was trying to focus on what was important, but Nancy had never been a blip on Lilly's radar. "It's amazing how much needs to be done to keep a library running smoothly. I find the days slip away from me before I'm ready for them to end. Especially with my assistant out of town."

"But I hear it hasn't kept you from nosing around." Lilly brought the cup to her lips and sipped.

"I'm sorry? I don't know what you're talking about."

"Everyone in Tipton knows you can't resist a good mystery. You've been like that since we were kids. Don't deny it. One of my clients mentioned having her license plate stolen off her pickup. Don't tell me you aren't trying to figure out who did it."

"I'm as curious as the next person about who is behind that. Do you have any ideas?"

Lilly shook her head somberly. "Not a one. But I'm paying more attention when I'm out. It's terrible what some people do. And for what?"

"Apparently there's money to be made in stolen plates. I think everyone in town would rest easier if the person is found."

"I'm sure. It would be nice to not have to worry about my plates being taken right off my vehicle."

Nancy nodded. "You haven't noticed anyone behaving suspiciously? No new faces? No new clients that make the hair on your neck stand?"

Lilly laughed. "You're quite the drama queen. I had no idea. To answer your question—no. How about you? I heard you approached a few business owners about installing security cameras."

Nancy cringed inwardly. She was supposed to let Carter do that but instead let her mouth run ahead of good sense. "I only asked a couple of friends I thought might want to help catch the person in the act. If we all band together, it will send a strong message that we won't stand for this in our town."

"True. I wish I could do something to help." Her face brightened. "Maybe I should put one outside my office too."

"That's a great idea." Nancy still hadn't figured out the purpose of this tête-à-tête, but her time was expired. "Speaking of offices, I need to open the library soon."

"Did you have any success finding gluten-free cookbooks?"

"Yes. I ordered two with excellent reviews. I'll give you a call when they arrive."

"You're the best, Nancy. I should head out also. I need to be at the bank when it opens." Worry lines creased Lilly's forehead.

"Everything okay?"

"Yes." Lilly smiled, but it didn't reach her eyes. "A

client is closing on a house today." She stood.

"Congratulations." Nancy wondered at the worry lines and fake smile. It seemed to her that closing on a house was a good thing, considering Lilly stood to make a nice profit. Nancy waved to Pepper on her way out. Pepper mouthed, *call me.* Did her friend have a lead on the license plate case? Or could she be curious about Lilly?

Nancy zipped her jacket to ward off the coolness of the fall morning. Having traded her heels for practical boots she would stick with walking. There was no reason to drive a couple of blocks. She glanced in the window of the florist shop and made a note to order a fall-colored bouquet. Most people couldn't understand why she bought herself flowers, but the truth was they made her happy.

It wouldn't be long until the storefront windows would be decked out in harvest colors. A zip of excitement zinged through her. The town held a harvest festival mid-October. It was a good time for all ages. She always manned the cakewalk, and after talking with Lilly, decided to include gluten free cupcakes this year. It seemed more and more people were either choosing to steer clear of gluten or had health issues that forced them to avoid it. She was thankful not to be included in that group. Life would not be the same without her weekly donut at Roaster's Coffee with Pepper.

A horn beeped. She followed the sound and waved to Lyle. Her mom worked with a good bunch of people. In many ways they'd become a surrogate family, and she'd do anything to help them—including finding bad guys.

She stood at the bottom of the concrete stairs that

led up to the library entrance and smiled, once again thankful she could make a living doing something she loved. A flash of red out of her peripheral vision grabbed her attention. She whipped her head toward the street. What had she seen? Everything appeared normal. Light traffic flowed. A few people walked along the sidewalk. A mother pushed a stroller in the direction of the park. Senses on alert, she stood still and listened for anything unusual.

A police car pulled up in front of the building. The window lowered. "Good morning, Nancy."

"Hi, Carter." She strode over to him and squatted beside the door at face level. "Everything okay?"

"I was going to ask you the same. You looked like something was wrong."

"Not wrong—puzzling." She explained about the flash of red.

He frowned. "The last time you told me a story like that, the license plate thief had struck."

Her stomach flipped. Maybe they'd get lucky and catch the person today. "Think I'll take a little walk before I open."

"Let me. I know this is a non-violent crime, but you can't be too careful."

"Fine. I should open on time anyway. Call me if you find anything."

At the end of his shift, Carter walked into the sheriff's department and immediately spotted Nancy through the glass window of her mom's office. Had something happened, or was this a friendly visit?

The vibe in the bullpen felt off. He spotted Lyle

across the room, ambled his direction, and cornered him by the water cooler. "What's going on?" He nodded toward the sheriff's office.

"I don't know. Nancy came in here about thirty minutes ago and the door's been closed since. Something is up, but I'm not sure what."

Should he interrupt? Probably not, then again, he had a good reason to do so. He strode to the office door and knocked.

Sheriff Daley motioned him inside. "Just the man we were waiting for. Have a seat."

"What's going on?" He took the chair beside Nancy, noting her anxious look.

"This was taped to the library door this afternoon. Nancy found it when she was locking up." She handed him a clear plastic evidence bag with a piece of paper inside. The letter was made up of words cut from a magazine. "Back off or else." He looked to Nancy. "This was addressed to you?"

She nodded. "Whoever left this made a huge error in judgment. No way will I back off now. In fact, I will devote all my free time to finding and stopping this reprobate scoundrel."

He chuckled. "Reprobate scoundrel, huh?"

She raised her chin and crossed her arms. "Yes."

He spotted a grin on the sheriff's face before she wiped it away. "When Nancy is upset, she tends to adopt the language of the most recent book she's read and loved."

"I see. Does she also behave like them? I'd like to be forewarned."

Nancy blew her breath out in a huff. "I'm sitting right here. I'd appreciate if you'd direct your questions to me. And no, I don't act like the characters in the books I read. But you have to admit the description fits. The thief is unprincipled and immoral."

"Agreed. And now he's taken it a step further by threatening you." Carter turned his attention to the sheriff. "Are you taking her off the case?"

She laced her fingers and rested them on her desk. "Nancy and I have discussed it, but for now she is officially still a consultant. However," she raised her voice slightly and focused her gaze on Nancy, "at the first sign of danger she'll call 911 and get to safety."

He clamped his teeth together to stop himself from protesting. He wanted Nancy off this case for her own safety whether or not she could take care of herself. But who was he to argue with the woman's mother? By the very nature of their relationship she would want to protect and keep her daughter safe.

"I promise I'll call for help if I need it. But you know I can take care of myself."

The sheriff nodded. "I'll see you at your place later. I have a few things to finish up here first."

"Okay." Nancy stood but hesitated at the door and glanced at him. "I take it you didn't see anything suspicious this morning?"

"Sorry. No. I meant to let you know, but my day got away from me."

"Okay. I guess we can catch up later."

When the door closed he focused his attention on his boss. "What didn't you tell Nancy?" He could see she wanted him to hang back, and there were only two reasons that he could think of—a break in the burglary cases or additional information regarding Nancy.

She opened the top drawer of her desk and pulled

out another evidence bag. "I received this two days ago."

He took the bag and noted the warning directed at Nancy. "She doesn't know?"

"No, and I don't want her to. I'm going to be straight with you. My daughter needs to be able to solve this case." She lowered her voice. "Between you and me, she blames herself for your predecessor's death. Frank was a good deputy, and the best detective I've ever worked with. He taught Nancy everything she knows, except what she's picked up from books. Nancy assisted him on several cases. He was on his way to investigate a tip she'd given him when he was in a fatal car crash."

"As it turned out, the tip was bogus."

Carter digested the information. "Why put her through this again? Why not let her drop into investigation obscurity?"

"Because it's in her blood. It's a piece of her. I don't want to see that part of my daughter die."

He sighed. He couldn't argue with her reasoning. Sheriff Daley knew the risks and had probably weighed the pros and cons. She clearly believed moving forward despite the threat was reasonable. "Why didn't you tell her about the threat made against her that you received?"

"I don't want her to know. When she received one directly, I felt it would be wise to stay quiet."

"It's not too late to tell her."

"I disagree. Now, you keep this between us. Understood?"

"Yes, ma'am. What am I supposed to do with this knowledge?"

"Watch out for her. Entrench yourself in her life. I don't want her to be alone. Ever. Work something out with Lyle. I'll be with her in the evenings and overnight."

"She's alone right now."

A smile touched her lips. "I have her covered."

He twisted his head to the side, stretching his neck, then released a pent-up breath. "Sounds like you have everything worked out."

"I do. See you tomorrow."

He stood and strode from her office. After he wrapped up some paperwork, he'd take off. This case was messed up, and he needed to figure out a plan. He wouldn't mind spending more time with Nancy. In fact, he'd hoped for it, but not under these circumstances.

An hour later, he sat in his house at the table eating with Gavin. "How was school?"

"Fine."

"Didn't your book club meet today?"

Gavin nodded.

"How many showed?"

"Five total. Including Maddie and me."

"That's great. I'm really happy for you and Maddie."

Gavin looked up from the burger he had his hand wrapped around. "Why are you so excited? It's only a book club. It's not like I got straight A's."

Carter chuckled. "I care about you, and I want to see you succeed in all areas of your life. Not only in academics." Hmm, maybe that's where the sheriff was coming from regarding Nancy. She wanted to help her daughter deal with misplaced guilt and not give up on a passion. He wanted to see his nephew find a place to fit in at his new school. Maybe it wasn't as complicated as he'd thought.

# Chapter Nine

THE FOLLOWING MONDAY AFTER NANCY FOUND the note taped to the library door, the smoke alarm in the library blared. The alarm was wired to alert the fire department automatically. She rushed through the stacks checking for anyone who might be ignoring the warning. It looked like everyone was out. She grabbed her coat and purse then hurried toward the exit. Smoke billowed out from underneath the storage door at the end of the hall. Her insides lurched, and she rushed out the front doors.

The first fire truck rolled to a stop. Nancy waved to Greg—the man in charge. He walked with purpose toward her.

"Is anyone inside?"

"Not that I could find." She sucked in her bottom lip. What if she'd missed someone?

"Okay. I need you to wait across the street."

"Why can't I wait here? I think the fire is contained to the storage room. I saw smoke coming from under the door." She crossed her arms. It wasn't like she'd get in the way or do something stupid.

His eyes narrowed. "Do as I say, Nancy, so I can do my job."

She turned and crossed the street. Shopkeepers stepped outside into the cool fall air.

The owner of the hardware store darted across the street and walked over to where she stood. "What's going on at the library, Nancy?"

"The smoke alarm went off. They're checking it out now."

"You didn't see a fire or smell smoke?"

"I didn't see a fire, but there was smoke coming from the storage room." She didn't want to admit she hadn't smelled any smoke. She woke up with a cold today, and her head and nose were congested. Somehow admitting out loud she didn't feel good felt like defeat. Worry niggled at the back of her mind. What if the storage room was a complete loss? Or worse yet, the fire fighters damaged any of the books.

Greg walked back outside accompanied by two other firefighters. He waved her over.

"Looks like the fire's out," she said to the storeowner. She jogged across the street then slowed. The grim look in Greg's face knotted her stomach. "What's wrong? Couldn't you get the fire out?"

"Someone set a storage bin filled with damp books on fire."

Her pulse jumped. "Arson? You mean not only was there a fire, but it was deliberately set?" How? Who would have done that? At least the fire had been set in the bin containing the books that had been left outside in the rain. She'd found them this morning. It appeared that they'd fallen from someone's vehicle since the book bag wasn't far away from where she'd found them laying haphazardly in the gutter. The damage was too bad to try and save them, so she'd dropped them in a bin to recycle later.

Who could have gained access to the storage room? A homeschool co-op of grade school children had come in today. Things had gotten busy for about an hour, but other than that, only a handful of patrons had been in.

"I noticed you have surveillance cameras. I'd like a copy."

"Of course. I can make one right now. How bad is the damage?"

"You got lucky. The fire mostly smoldered which caused the smoke that set off the alarm. The loss is minimal, all things considered. I'm surprised you or anyone else didn't smell it."

"Me too." Why hadn't anyone said anything? The last patron had left shortly before the alarm went off. Maybe it wasn't strong enough or maybe she had a cold too. Nancy sneezed as if on cue.

"Bless you."

"Thanks. I'll go make that copy right now. I can send it to you if that's okay."

"Sure."

A sheriff's car pulled up behind the fire truck. It was about time one of them showed up. She thought for sure her mom would have been here before the fire trucks. She must be out in the countryside today.

Carter's long stride carried him closer to Nancy. Concern filled his eyes. "What happened?" he asked as he stopped beside them.

"We haven't met." The fire captain held out his hand. "I'm Greg Walker."

"Carter Malone. You're the Captain?"

He nodded. "The fire appears to have been started in the storage room. The arson investigator is on her way so we'll know for certain what happened, but it appears someone started a fire in the recycle bin."

"You're certain it was arson?"

"Yes."

A grim look covered Carter's face. "Okay. I'll be in

touch. Thanks." He turned his attention to Nancy. "We need to talk."

"Okay." Carter had been hanging around more this past week, so she wasn't surprised to see him, but his serious voice left her feeling uneasy. This had to be related to the license plate case, but how?

Concern for Nancy gripped Carter. Her face was pasty white. "Hang in there, Nancy. Let's go take a seat." He rested a hand on her elbow and guided her away from the gathering crowd of onlookers to a private bench situated to the side of the library.

He gently tugged her down beside him on the stone bench that faced the statues. "You okay?"

"Someone either tried to kill me, or send a message, knowing the smoke alarm would go off long before my life was in danger. No, I'm not okay." She looked at him, and anger filled her eyes. "What are we going to do?"

Relief surged though him—she was a fighter. For a minute he thought she would crumble. Her strength intrigued and impressed him. "We're going to watch the security footage and go from there. Then you're going to make sure you're never alone until this is over." Between Lyle, himself and her mother, they'd tried to keep an eye on her, but things were different now. "This person has shown they mean business and that concerns me."

"Yeah. Me too. What bothers me the most is we are talking about license plates. The response is overkill. No pun intended."

He chuckled. "None taken, and I agree. Could this be personal?"

Her brow furrowed. "Do I think someone has something against me? I don't know."

"I assume your consulting has led to arrests."

She nodded. "But I've never had to testify. I pass my intel on to the authorities, which allows me to keep my anonymity. Are you suggesting this is an act of revenge for something I've done?"

"Maybe, but that feels like a stretch. The threatening note specifically told you to back off the license plate investigation. Since you haven't altered your behavior, this could be a message that they mean business."

"Believe it or not, I like that theory better." She stood. "Let's go inside, watch the video, and see who I may have missed. I wish I had cameras in the hall that lead to the storage room. It never occurred to me it was necessary."

He walked beside her as they made their way inside the library. "Maybe you should close while the investigation is going on."

"Right." She turned and put the closed sign on the door. "I can't lock up though, or the arson investigator won't be able to enter."

"I'll watch for him. Lock up." He told dispatch what was going on and asked to be notified when the investigator arrived. Then he went over to Nancy's desk where she sat staring at the computer screen. "You see anything?"

"Nothing I didn't expect. I started from this morning watching from eight o'clock on."

"This will take the rest of the day at this rate. Can you make me a copy?"

"Already done. I emailed the file to you and Captain

Walker. I can also fast forward through this." She increased the speed and paused every time a person came into view. She wrote the person's name down or a description if she didn't know it.

A knock sounded on the library door. "I'll see who it is." Carter hustled toward the door. "It's Gloria," he said over his shoulder.

A moment later, Nancy paused beside him. "I wonder what she wants. I don't imagine you're her favorite person."

"Good point. Think I'll hang back and let you talk with her." Gloria wasn't his favorite person either, and he'd rather avoid her when possible. Her eccentric nature was over-the-top irritating. "Tell her the library is closed."

Nancy shot him a look of annoyance then walked to the door. She opened it slightly. "I'm sorry, Gloria, but the library is closed for the rest of the day."

"What happened? I heard there was a fire."

"You heard correctly, but everything is fine now."

Gloria rested a hand at her waist. "Nancy Daley, you know I'm a huge supporter of this library, and I want to know what happened."

Nancy looked over her shoulder toward him. Was she asking for his help? That was a first. He stepped forward. "Ms. Davis, we can't comment on the events of today until the investigation is complete. At that time the public will be informed."

Gloria waved a finger. "I'm not the public." She focused a hard look on Nancy. "I thought we were friends. I guess I was wrong."

"This has nothing to do with friendship. My hands are tied. Please understand, Gloria."

Her friend's face softened. "When you know something, call me." She pivoted and marched away.

Nancy sighed and turned to face Carter. "Thanks. I wasn't sure what I could or couldn't say."

"Technically, you could have told her. I don't think it would've been an issue."

"Says the man who hasn't experienced the power of the Tipton gossip train. I consider Gloria a friend, but she likes to talk." She returned to her desk with slumped shoulders. "I don't know if solving this case is worth all of this." Her sad eyes spoke to her discouragement. "Is it really such a big deal if a few license plates disappear from time to time? What if someone had been hurt today? If that smoke alarm had been tampered with, and the fire had left the confines of the storage room, it could have been very serious." She ended with a cough.

He thought about her mother's comment. At first, he had a hard time believing Nancy would blame herself for his predecessor's death, but not any longer. "How about you get out of here? I'll stick around and let in the arson investigator. You go home and rest. You're clearly not feeling well."

"I don't know. The library is my responsibility."

His heart warmed toward her. He wanted nothing more than to be with her and ensure she was okay but going home was best. Her mom could probably head out early to be with her. "I promise to come by your place later to give you an update. Plus, I'm only a phone call away if you can't wait."

The look on her face said no way was she leaving, but then the fight left her. "Fine." She was worse off than he'd realized. He wanted to encourage her, but at the same time he longed to keep her safe.

Nancy slipped into her coat and grabbed her purse. "I do feel rotten today. Maybe a nap is a good idea."

He accompanied her to the door then locked up behind her and pulled out his cell. He pressed his first contact.

Lyle answered on the second ring. "Carter, what do you know?"

"Nothing yet. I sent Nancy home." He watched from the window as she trudged down the stairs. "Will you make sure she gets there safely?"

"Already on it. I saw her leave the building as I was passing by."

"Good. Will you also let the sheriff know she's at home alone?"

"Will do."

Carter stuffed his phone away. Confident Nancy would be taken care of, he continued viewing the video feed to see if anyone raised suspicion. One of the people who entered this building today set the fire, and once he found that person, he'd probably find the thief.

Two hours later, he had his answer about the cause of the fire—arson. It had been started with a smoke bomb. It appeared whoever committed the act only wanted to stir up a ruckus—no one was supposed to get hurt. He rested easier with that knowledge as he locked up and headed out.

An hour later, he stood outside Nancy's home holding a bag with a container of soup inside from BLB. He'd heard they made great chicken soup. Strange, considering it was a burger joint, but after the third person he asked about chicken soup said to get it there, he'd listened.

He knocked on the door and waited, straining to hear footsteps, but he only heard silence. Had the sheriff not come to be with her daughter? He knocked again, harder this time. Nancy's car was in the driveway, so she had to be here. He peered through the window in the door and spotted her face down on the floor. "Nancy!"

# Chapter Ten

CARTER TRIED THE DOORKNOB TO NANCY'S HOUSE—open. His pulse raced as he pulled out his service weapon. Had he interrupted her attacker? He crept inside. Silence. His gut wrenched at the site of Nancy. He knelt beside her, senses on alert, as she lay on her stomach about five feet from the front door. He checked her pulse—normal—but she was warm to the touch—feverish. He cleared the rooms in the remainder of the house to make sure no one lurked behind a closed door, shower curtain, or under a bed.

Satisfied they were alone, he rushed back to Nancy. She looked the same as when he'd first spotted her. Had she fallen asleep on the floor? "Nancy," he said softly.

"Mmm."

He jiggled her shoulder. "Nancy, wake up."

She groaned and slowly opened one eye. Gasping, she pushed up. "Whoa." She closed her eyes and held her head. "Remind me not to move fast." She sat there with her eyes closed a moment then opened them.

"Do you need help?"

"Might be a good idea. I'm so congested I keep getting light headed. The room was spinning earlier, I think I must have passed out and fallen. When I came to, I decided it'd be safer to lay here for a little bit. I guess I fell asleep. I can't believe how quickly this came on. I felt under the weather at work, but within an hour of being home this hit me full force."

No wonder she agreed so easily to go home and wait for word about the fire. He stood and offered her a hand.

She grasped it, allowing him to pull her up. She gripped his forearms and closed her eyes. "I hate this."

"You okay?"

"I will be." She finally opened her eyes and released her grip on him. "Let's sit."

"I brought chicken noodle soup from BLB."

Her face lit. "Seriously? That's so sweet. You're growing on me, Carter. I take back every bad thought I had about you."

He chuckled. "That must be your fever talking."

"Maybe, but I don't think so."

He had strong doubts she'd be saying that if she weren't feverish. "Where do you want to eat?"

"The couch." She settled onto the comfortable-looking contemporary sofa.

He sat facing her on the cushioned ottoman that doubled as a coffee table and pulled out the soup, a plastic spoon, and napkins. "Here you go."

"Thanks." She pried off the lid and breathed in the steam. "How'd you know BLB has the best soup in town?"

"Everyone I asked recommend the place."

"Would you like some before I dig in?"

"No thanks. That's for you." He'd grabbed a couple burgers while he was there. Hopefully they would still be good by the time he got home. Gavin wouldn't appreciate a soggy bun and cold meat.

"You're my hero." She batted her lashes.

"Are you flirting with me?"

"I think I am." She sounded shocked. "It must be the fever. I won't let it happen again."

He chuckled. "I don't mind."

She raised a brow as she spooned soup into her mouth. "I thought I had a cold this morning, but I think it might be the flu. You probably should go. I don't want to make you sick."

"It's a little early for flu season, isn't it?"

She shrugged. "Says the man who isn't sick. Thank you for bringing this, but you really should go. I'll be fine."

He didn't want to leave her because clearly, she wasn't okay; however, if staying was going to upset her, he'd do as she asked. "I'll go, but before I do, would you like to know the arson investigator's conclusion?"

"I already do. The arson investigator called an hour ago. I got up to answer the phone and decided the couch was too far away."

He chuckled. Everything was beginning to fall into place. "Okay. I'll see myself out." He stood and headed for the door. He'd sit outside in his car until her mother arrived. No way would he leave her alone now.

"Don't lock it."

"Why not?"

"If anyone else comes over I don't want to get up to answer. This way I can holler for them to come in."

He shook his head. "Someone set off a smoke bomb today to send you a warning, and you're comfortable leaving your house unlocked?" He'd figured it was an oversight, not deliberate, when he was able to enter through the unlocked door.

"When you put it like that, no. Lock up please."

He nodded and did as she asked before closing the door. Sheriff Daley stopped beside Nancy's car in the driveway. He ambled over to the hood of her car.

She got out. "What brings you by, Carter?"

"Nancy is sick. I brought her chicken soup."

"That was nice of you. I didn't realize she was ill. I wanted to get here sooner, but it was a busy day."

"Lyle called you?"

She nodded. "If I'd known Nancy was sick, I would have worked from here. Thanks for looking after her, Carter. You're a good man." She turned and muttered, "if only my daughter could see that."

What was that about? Nancy didn't think he was a bad man, did she? Heat crept up his neck. Why would she think that? Other than their early-on encounter at Gloria's house, things had gone well between them. He shook off the thought. He must have heard her mom wrong.

The sheriff closed the car door then went to the trunk and pulled out a suitcase.

"Are you sleeping over?" Carter asked.

She kept her voice low. "After the notes and the fire, you bet. That's my daughter, and no one is going to hurt her."

"Good. By the way, I found her sleeping on the floor when I arrived. She said she'd been dizzy and thinks she passed out. The door was unlocked."

The sheriff frowned. "On the floor? Unlocked? Looks like I'm here not a moment too soon. Thanks for stopping by."

"Sure thing." Dismissed, he went on his way. He got behind the wheel of his car and headed home. Thankfully his place was only a couple of streets over. Dealing with a rash of burglaries had been taking much of his time, but finding whoever dropped that smoke bomb jumped to the top of his priority list.

"I don't need a babysitter." Nancy couldn't believe her mother had invited herself over and planned on staying indefinitely. What was up with that?

"Of course, you don't." Her mom sat beside her on the couch. "Think of it as doing your mother a favor."

"I don't understand." She set the soup Carter had brought on the ottoman then crossed her arms.

"It's like this. You're sick, and it makes me feel good to take care of you."

"Oh. So that's why you're here? Because I'm sick?"

Mom looked away from her. "Partly. But let's stick with that for now."

Nancy's mom had never been a mother who hovered and had to be involved in every aspect of her life. She'd taught Nancy to be independent and self-sufficient. "Are you worried because of the fire?"

"That's part of my concern. Whoever sent that note means business, and you're in no condition to take care of trouble should it arise."

Nancy couldn't argue that fact, considering she'd chosen to nap on the floor rather than fight the lightheadedness and get to the couch to rest. "This person has you worried?" If she hadn't already been nauseous she would be now. Her mom wasn't the worrying type.

Mom ignored her question and stood. "Would you like something to drink?"

"Yes. Water please."

Mom headed to the kitchen. "I saw Carter as he was leaving. There anything going on between the two of you?"

Nancy's heart skipped a beat at the thought. "He only brought me soup. We aren't even friends, so don't get all excited." Okay, that wasn't exactly the truth. A week ago, yes, now...not so much. Carter seemed to be a great guy. Sure, they'd gotten off to a rocky beginning, and her first impressions of him were negative, but he was a good man. The thought startled her. She tucked it away for now.

Mom peered around the corner. "You're not friends?" Confusion covered her face.

"Maybe that was a stretch. He's been popping in on my life a lot this past week, and we're getting to know one another. That being said, there is nothing going on between us." She knew what her mom was thinking. "We're two professionals working on a case together." And not doing a very good job either, considering the perp was still at large.

"So there's no attraction?" Her mom walked back into the room and sat in the recliner.

Was she seriously having this conversation with her mother? Her face heated. They never talked like this. She knew her mom, and this line of questioning wouldn't go away unless she laid things out clearly. "He's actually a nice guy who I wouldn't mind being friends with." Who was she kidding? He had won her over with the soup. She wouldn't mind going out with him and seeing where things went. However, considering the timing of when Carter started inserting himself into her life, she wondered if he was only doing what he considered to be his job—protect her from any threat. No matter. Her solo life suited her just fine—no man needed, but she wouldn't mind if he was sincere in his interest. Just because she didn't *need* a man in her life didn't mean she wouldn't enjoy one. Especially one as thoughtful as Carter.

"Not what I asked."

A knock sounded on her door. *Whew.* Saved by the knock. Hopefully Mom would forget about this conversation and move on. She needed time to consider where her head was and thinking a cold-foggy brain was not a good idea.

Mom stood. "Are you expecting company?"

"It's probably my neighbor Anna. We've been walking together. Will you tell her I'm sick?" She had begun to look forward to their girl talk while they walked and would miss it this evening, but she didn't want to make Anna sick.

Mom gave her friend the message then returned to the recliner. "I noticed the pickings in your fridge are slim. I'll get groceries on my way home from work tomorrow."

Nancy only nodded. She had no more energy. This bug had hit hard and fast. Maybe it would go away as fast as it'd come. "I'm going to bed. Maybe I can sleep this off."

"Good idea. What will you do about the library if you're still sick in the morning?"

"I guess Tara will have to get the key from you and run it on her own." Tara James worked half-time during the busier hours. But Nancy had been running the library solo for the past few weeks since Tara had been out of state taking care of her sick mother. Thank goodness she was scheduled to be back tomorrow and could be called in early if necessary.

Nancy headed to her room and fifteen minutes later, clothed in her Wonder Woman pajamas, she snuggled under the sheets. After what seemed like only minutes, she awoke to her mother shaking her shoulder. "What's wrong?" She pried her eyes open and squinted at the light her mom must have turned on.

"I have to leave for work soon and wanted to make sure you were up before I left."

"Mom, I've been on my own for five years. I know how to wake myself and get myself to work on time."

"I know, but I also wanted to see how you're feeling."

Her headache was gone, and her body no longer hurt. Come to think of it, she was hungry. "I'm much better. I'll see you tonight. Are you still planning to grocery shop?"

"Yes."

"Okay. Thanks. If I'm not here when you arrive, don't panic." Mom hadn't fooled her—she was worried about her safety. Although she didn't like it, having her mother here was probably a good idea. Her thoughts shifted to the case. She needed to wrap it up soon, or something would have to change. She liked her independence and having her mom under the same roof would get old fast. If only she could figure out what they were missing.

# Chapter Eleven

THE DAY AFTER THE FIRE, NANCY sat at her desk in the library going through the list she created of people who had been in the day before. The scent of smoke lingered in the air, making her all the more determined to find who did it.

"What's the frown about?"

Nancy looked up. "Hi, Lilly. What brings you by two days in a row?"

She held up the cookbook she'd picked up yesterday. "This one was a dud. The recipes are too complicated and required a lot of ingredients I don't have on hand."

Nancy frowned. "That's disappointing. It had great reviews. I hope the other one was good." She reached for it and put it in her to-be-checked-in stack.

"I haven't had time to peruse it yet." She turned around in a circle and appeared to be searching for something. "I heard there was a fire here yesterday, but it looks like I heard wrong. Everything seems normal." She sniffed. "Then again, it does have an interesting odor."

"You heard right, but it was only a small fire. All the books are safe." She'd been answering questions since she arrived to open the library this morning. A small crowd had been waiting for her. They'd heard about the fire too and wanted to see the library for themselves. They actually seemed disappointed that there was nothing to see. She didn't take anyone to the storage room.

Granted, most of the people who'd stopped in only wanted to talk. Now she was talked out and couldn't wait for Tara to get here so she could take a break. Normally she could make it through the day with no problem, but she must be recovering from yesterday. At least she felt better today.

"I'm glad the library wasn't damaged," Lilly said. "Do they know the cause?"

Tara breezed in the front door.

Nancy stood. "You're here. Excuse me, Lilly." She rushed around her desk to the assistant librarian and gave her a quick hug.

Shock covered Tara's face. "That was...unexpected."

Nancy grinned. "I'm very happy you're back. I'd forgotten how difficult running this place by myself can be. How's your mom?"

"She's hanging in there. My sister took over her care so I could come home." She looked around the space. "Looks the same."

"Pretty much. Go clock in, then I'll get you up to speed."

Lilly waved. "'Bye, Nancy."

"See you around, Lilly."

"That's the local real estate agent, right?" Tara asked.

"Yes. Are you looking to buy or sell?"

"Not really. I'm trying to do a better job placing people. You know how I struggle with names."

Nancy nodded. "Sure do. It's really great having you back." Even though Tara hadn't grown up in Tipton, she had fit in like she'd lived here her entire life.

Tara chuckled. "So you said."

Nancy tucked her list of names into her purse. There was no reason to worry Tara with this. Besides her trouble remembering names, she wouldn't know who the majority of the people were anyhow, based solely on a name.

Tara returned from the private office then plopped down beside her. "It's so good to be back. I've missed Tipton and the library. This place soothes my frayed nerves. How did you handle running this place on your own? I hope it wasn't too awful."

"There were moments that challenged me, but for the most part, it's been pretty quiet."

"Good. What have I missed?" Tara asked as she checked in the returned books then placed them on a wheeled cart.

The perfect opening—so much for acclimating. "Well, since you asked, we had a small incident yesterday." She filled Tara in on the past few weeks including the new deputy, however she left out the part about consulting with him regarding the license plate case. She trusted Tara, but that was a need to know, and she didn't.

"That's crazy. Are there any suspects?"

An entire list, but none of them seemed plausible. Keeping her voice low, she filled Tara in on the surveillance cameras and the fire.

"I can't understand why anyone would do that." She frowned. "Do you think it was one of the homeschool kids?"

"No way. They were all young and very well behaved. If I had to guess, I'd say a teenager did it, but no teens are visible on the recording during the time in question."

"Doesn't mean one didn't sneak in the back door."

"I always keep it locked."

"You sure about that? Remember the deadbolt on that door is tricky. Even though it appears to have locked, you have to check to make sure it actually slides into place."

Tara was right. Nancy jumped up. "Be right back." She raced to the back door and sure enough, it wasn't locked. There went the usefulness of the video. Whoever set the fire probably snuck in through the back door, and she had been none the wiser. Had someone sneaked back and unlocked it, or had she overlooked it when closing up? All that time wasted! She marched back to her desk. "It wasn't bolted."

Tara frowned. "For once, I hoped to be wrong. What's next?"

"I'm working on that."

"Okay then. That's my cue to get to work." Tara pushed the cart away while Nancy called a locksmith. That door needed to be fixed pronto. After scheduling an appointment for the lock repair, she finished up a few tasks while she waited on Tara to finish her work. She looked toward the stacks where Tara still shelved books. Maybe she should help. No, she could wait for Tara to get done and then head out. Besides, this year's budget awaited her attention. She pulled the spreadsheet up on her computer and sighed. Numbers were not her favorite thing, and her mind was too distracted to concentrate on them. Instead, she updated the website to include the various fall activities the library was hosting.

Thirty minutes later, Tara meandered over. "You're still here?"

"I was waiting for you to finish shelving books."

Tara's faced turned a pretty shade of pink. "I'm sorry, I didn't realize you were waiting and stopped to help someone find a book. Then someone else needed help too."

Nancy looked around. There was a buzz in the air. When had everyone come in? She must have been very focused on the computer. And here she'd thought she couldn't concentrate. Her ability to block out the world around her didn't bode well for her investigative skills.

"Are you okay?" Tara asked.

"Yes, sorry. I was lost in my thoughts. Will you be fine on your own for about an hour?"

"Absolutely. Don't worry about a thing. I've got this."

"Okay. If you need me shoot me a text. I won't be far away."

"Will do."

Nancy grabbed her coat and purse then headed for the exit. She had enough time to go see Pepper and get back before the locksmith arrived. As she stepped outside, the cool fall air caused her to tuck her fingers inside the sleeves of her coat. Would this be a cold winter like last year? She hoped not. Although she loved this time of year, snow and ice made for some hectic days last year.

"What's your hurry?"

Her heart skipped a beat at the sound of the familiar male voice. She looked over her shoulder as she made her way along the sidewalk then stopped and smiled. "Hi, Carter. I'm surprised to see you here."

"I was on my way to see you when I spotted you charging from the library. I had to hustle to catch up."

"Speaking of hustling, do you mind if we walk and talk?" Did he have news about the arson? She began walking without waiting for his reply, knowing he'd acquiesce.

"Actually, we do have a suspect."

She slowed. "Really?" In truth she expected the police to be as clueless as she was. Good thing she was wrong. "Who?"

He lowered his voice and leaned in. "Tara James."

Nancy gasped. "Impossible." She shook her head. "There's absolutely no way Tara had anything to do with this. I would stake my reputation as a sleuth on it."

"Evidence doesn't lie."

"What evidence?"

"A witness spotted Tara alongside the library yesterday about an hour before the smoke alarm went off."

"That's not evidence. That's a coincidence. Tara is a trusted employee, and I consider her a friend. She would never do something like that. Keep looking, Carter. Tara is innocent."

"I did a little checking around and learned that she returned to town several days ago, yet didn't come back to work until today. Did your *friend* tell you that?"

Nancy bit the inside of her cheek. "No. But that's irrelevant. I thought the theory was that the person who sent the letter set the fire. Tara couldn't have done it. She's been out of town for several weeks. All of this began after she left to take care of her mom." Nancy gave him a curt nod then continued walking toward Roaster's Coffee.

Carter kept pace beside her. "Okay. Let's say I'm wrong and you're right. Why do you think Tara was lurking by the library, and why didn't she let on to you that she came back to town sooner than expected?"

She tossed up her hands. "I don't know, Carter. But I do know she's not guilty of what you accused her, and I can't believe anyone in this town would suggest she would do something like that."

He cleared his throat. "Well... actually, no one accused her. I drew my own conclusion."

She stopped outside the door of the coffee shop. "I have a few theories I'd like to run by you. When can we meet again?"

"Why not come for dinner at my place?"

She hesitated. People were going to start talking if they saw her car parked at his place too often. Then again, let them talk, she was done caring.

"Gavin's friend Maddie will be there too, but we can find a private place to talk."

"Okay. What time?"

"Six thirty."

"Sounds good. See you later." That would give her plenty of time to walk with Anna and get cleaned up after.

Pepper smiled and waved when she spotted her. "This is a surprise. What's up?"

"Can't a girl visit her friend for lunch for no reason?"

"Sure. But not Nancy Daley."

Nancy chuckled. Pepper knew her too well. "Fine. You're right, but I'm here for lunch too. I'd like the cobb salad and water."

"Coming up." Pepper sent the order to the kitchen. "I'll bring it out to you and we can talk."

Nancy nodded then found the most out-of-the-way seat she could and gathered her thoughts. Seeing Carter had almost made her forget her purpose for coming here. There was something about that man that sent her mind to the clouds lately. La-la land was not where her thoughts needed to be.

"Here you go." Pepper placed the salad in front of Nancy along with a glass of ice water. "Now what's going on?"

"I'm sure you heard about the fire at the library."

Pepper nodded.

"I was hoping you might have an idea about who set it."

Pepper frowned. "Everyone is talking about it." She leaned in. "Most people think it was a kid."

"A child-kid or a teenager?"

"A teen."

"Did anyone see anything?"

"Not that I've heard."

"Okay." She'd suggest to Carter to get a copy of the school attendance record to see who skipped class around that time. That would narrow the suspects, especially if they could somehow tie the license plate thefts with the arson. "Why does everyone think a kid is responsible?"

"Why would an adult do something like that? It's a juvenile prank."

"Hmm." Nancy tapped her chin. She would have the same thought if she hadn't received the letter from the thief. Then again, maybe they were onto something. The prank was juvenile, so did that confirm they were looking for a teenage thief? "I better eat this so I can get back to work." She took a big bite, barely tasting the food as her mind raced with possibilities.

"Nancy? Did you hear me?" Pepper asked.

"No. Sorry."

"I said there's a rumor going around that you and Carter are an item."

She laughed. "Figures. I knew it would happen sooner or later."

"Is it true?" Surprise filled her voice.

"You know I'd tell you if there was anything to tell?"

"Sure, but you made me think twice for a minute. Anyway, I wanted you to know so you wouldn't be blindsided if it ever comes up."

"Thanks."

"Guess I'll leave you to your meal. See you Friday."

Nancy nodded and placed another bite into her mouth. With all that was going on in this town one would think they would be too distracted to create false news. After all, she often hung out with cops. Deputy Malone was an extremely handsome single cop who was bound and determined to find the arsonist, and fast. She only hoped he'd find the perp before he struck again.

# Chapter Twelve

CARTER ROLLED HIS NECK TO RELEASE pent-up tension as he sat shoulder to shoulder with Nancy on his porch swing. Gavin and Maddie were in the kitchen, working on English homework. The house was too small to talk freely inside. "While you were at Roaster's, I went back to the library and questioned Tara."

Nancy's head whipped in his direction. "Even after I told you she was innocent?" She crossed her arms and faced forward. "No wonder Tara seemed out of sorts when I returned. I chalked it up to it being her first day back."

"You of all people know I have to follow up on leads. I can't simply take your word for it, Nancy." He kept his voice low, not wanting any passersby to overhear.

She scooted as far away from him as possible. "So what'd she say?"

Fall evenings in Oregon were chillier than he was accustomed to, and cold seeped through his jacket. "That she was merely walking by the library, and she hadn't come to work sooner because she had things to do after being gone."

"Sounds logical to me."

"Yeah. She's off my suspect list." At least officially, but something about Tara bothered him.

"Good. So what's going on with you and Gavin? He seemed a little cold toward you tonight."

Speaking of cold. Nancy still sat as far from him as

possible. "If we're going to sit out here, you need to come closer or we're both going to freeze."

She chuckled. "Fine. I forget you aren't used to this weather." She slid over until their shoulders touched. "Better?"

"N-not yet." His teeth chattered.

"Oh, my goodness. You really are cold. Give me your hands." She wrapped hers around his. "About Gavin?"

Her warmth shot chills up his arms. He willed himself to stop shivering from the cold as well as her touch. Nancy had an effect on him no other woman had ever had. He pushed aside the thought and focused on her question. "He's still mad at me about not letting him hang out with Maddie downtown at night."

"Oh. But she's here now, so what's the problem?"

"I believe we're having a power struggle."

"Ah. I see. Do you have any more clues about the thief?"

"Nothing firm. I talked to a woman today who had a license plate turn up missing while her vehicle was parked in her driveway. She stated a few kids had come over from the high school to rake leaves and noticed it was missing after they left."

"That fits what we were thinking." Excitement filled her voice. "All we need are their names, and then you can check their alibis about where they were during one of the other incidents."

He'd had the same thought except for one problem. "The woman is elderly and can't remember who was there."

"And she drives?"

"No. Her husband does, but he was taking a nap at that time. Apparently, it didn't take more than thirty minutes to complete the job."

"What about their neighbors? This is a small town. Surely someone remembers one of them."

He shook his head. "They live outside of town—no close neighbors."

"Stink. Okay, so it appears our perpetrator could be a teenager. Were they boys or girls?"

"Both."

"Figures. Did they represent one of the clubs at the school, or a team?"

"Good question. I'll find out. And once I do, I'll be sure to ask them if anyone not part of their group showed up."

"Good plan. Check with the school office. Someone there would more than likely be able to find out if any groups were doing community service or a fundraiser."

He should have thought of that. "Have you discovered anything new?"

"No. To be honest, I'm frustrated with this case. Every time I think I'm onto something, it turns out to be a dead end."

He shared her frustration. "We'll find whoever is behind all of this. They're going to slip up sooner or later and when they do—"

"We'll nab 'em," she said dramatically.

"Right." Though he bit back a grin at her enthusiasm, he had no intention of allowing Nancy anywhere near this person when it came time to make an arrest. She'd already been threatened, and he would not put her in danger if he could avoid doing so.

"I've been running through all the different clues that have been left—"

"Which clues?" He rested his arm along the back of

the swing. It seemed to him, other than knowing the approximate height and body shape of the perpetrator, they had little to go on.

"I was about to tell you. I believe the letter was a clue. The person reads or subscribes to magazines."

"Or they live in a home with someone else who does."

She frowned. "Good point. As I was saying, the person probably didn't come up with that idea on his— or her—own. I think it's safe to say he enjoys watching TV or movies. We also know this person is watching me." She shivered.

He doubted it was from the cold. "Have you noticed anyone?"

"Maybe. There were two instances when I spotted someone darting away as if they didn't want me to see them."

"I remember that. Whoever he was he's quick on his feet."

"So probably a young person."

"Not necessarily. I've chased several older people who were tough to catch." He grinned as he watched her process. "What else have you noted?"

She sat up straight. "I don't know why I didn't think of this before, but when I've spotted those people it was during school hours. There goes my theory about the culprit being a teenager."

"He could've been skipping class or had a release period."

She sighed and slumped back. "It feels like all we do is go around and around. It's frustrating."

The defeat in her voice concerned him. He wanted her to be safe and off the case altogether. Yet, it appeared when she worked a case she was extra vigilant about safety. "Yes, but together, we'll figure this out." He sensed her gaze on him and turned her way. Their faces were only a breath apart. "What?"

"I was thinking about how you've changed since you were first told you had to work with me on this." She grinned then faced forward.

He took a deep breath then let it out slowly. "You've grown on me. Working with you helps me to see things differently."

"A lot of good it's done, all things considered."

He nudged his shoulder into hers. "Where's this coming from?"

"I don't know. I guess it's getting to me that someone threatened me. It hit me tonight that I'm being watched, and I don't like it."

His gut tightened. Her mother assured him Nancy could take care of herself, but it sounded like she didn't have the stomach for danger he'd assumed she had. "I get that. Anyone would feel that way, but you also have people watching out for you. One of us is bound to spot the perp. The fact that we haven't yet, tells me whoever it is doesn't watch you 24/7. Which takes me back to my teenager theory."

"Or it could be someone with a job."

"And there you go again, making me think about things differently."

She chuckled. "Thanks."

"For what?"

"Making me feel better. I was having a pity party, but it's over now."

He grinned. "Glad to hear it. How about we head inside and check on Gavin and Maddie? They've been quiet."

"Good idea." She stood. The light from the house sconce gave her an angelic glow. He reached out and touched her hair.

"Is there something in it?" Nancy reached up and touched her hair.

He shook his head and pulled his hand away. "No, sorry. The light...er...never mind." He turned and went inside his house. What was wrong with him? No more quiet talks on the front porch with Nancy—it messed with his mind.

She followed him inside and closed the door. A bemused look covered her face. "Where do you think they are?"

Right. He'd forgotten they were checking on the kids. "Good question." He trotted up the stairs and strode to Gavin's room. He stopped in the doorway. They sat side-by-side at his desk, and by the look of it they were working on a project. "I expected you to be downstairs." He sent a pointed look at his nephew. "How's it going?" He'd have a word with him later about staying downstairs. Girls weren't allowed in Gavin's room, even to study.

Gavin looked over his shoulder. "Good. We are about finished. Is it okay if I walk Maddie home? She lives around the block, so it's not too far."

"Sure." He couldn't help grinning. It looked like his nephew was turning into a gentleman. Nancy tugged on Carter's arm, grabbing his attention. He followed her downstairs to the living room. "What's up?"

"Nothing. But you looked a little silly standing there grinning." She raised an eyebrow.

"Whatever."

She laughed. "You sound like them." She raised a thumb toward Gavin's room.

"You would too, if you were around a teenager so much."

"Maybe. It sounds like he's not mad at you anymore."

"Now that you mention it, things do seem to have thawed."

"I'm glad." She headed for the door.

"I'll walk you to your car."

"You don't have to."

"I want to." Besides the fact he didn't want her out there alone, he really did want to be with her a bit longer.

"Suit yourself." She shouldered her purse and headed back outside.

Cold air washed over him. "I'm not sure I'll ever get used to Oregon weather."

"You will eventually. At least, most people do. You're lucky it hasn't been super rainy. Combine the rain with the cold, and then you'll really miss the California sunshine." She stopped beside her car and pulled open the driver's door, holding it between them as if to shield herself from him.

"Drive safely."

"Always."

"Right," he said slowly. He raised a brow, recalling his first experience with her driving. The woman drove like a racecar driver.

She chuckled. "Oh, stop. I'm a good driver."

"Good night, Nancy." He waited for her to slip behind the wheel then closed the door. From the sidewalk he watched her drive away. Across the street he heard footsteps, then a car door closed. He stepped into the shadows and waited.

Nancy couldn't get her mind off of Carter. Something was different about him tonight, but she couldn't place what. Or maybe she couldn't reconcile what she thought she saw with what she knew. Carter acted like a man smitten, but that was impossible, at least where she was concerned. Yes, he'd admitted he enjoyed discussing the case with her, but there was a canyon between that and what she thought she saw on his face tonight when he touched her hair.

*Lord, what's going on? I know You have everything in control, but right now it doesn't feel like it. This case has me concerned, and You know how I feel about men. It's not that I don't desire to be loved, but I'm not sure I'm capable of trusting my heart to a man. Not after what my dad did to Mom and me.*

Headlights in her rearview mirror grabbed her attention. Where had that car come from? She hadn't noticed it behind her until now, and she was an observant driver. Could it have had the lights off? The car inched closer. She pushed harder on the gas pedal, pulling away from the tailgater. The car sped closer. "Come on, back off." Butterflies filled her stomach. What if this wasn't simply a bad driver? What if this was the same person who sent the note?

She floored the gas, passing her house. Her mom's car sat in the driveway. Using Bluetooth, she called her mom. "Someone's following me."

"You sure?"

She glanced in her rearview mirror again—no

headlights. "Yes! But it's gone now. I'm positive he was following me."

"You get a look at the driver?" Mom asked with surprise in her tone.

"No. But I think he was driving a pickup. I couldn't tell for sure."

"Where are you?"

"A few blocks south of the house. I'll turn around and head back."

"Okay. Be careful. Stay on the phone with me."

Nancy slowed and did a three-point turn in the middle of the road then headed toward home. A few minutes later, she spotted her mom standing in the driveway. Nancy pulled in and got out. She took several calming breaths before walking over to her mother who now waited beside the hood.

"You okay?"

"I'm fine, but we better hurry up and catch this guy."

"Let's get inside. Who knows what this person is capable of?" Mom waited for her to lead the way.

Once inside, Nancy melted into the couch.

Mom sat in the recliner wearing a frown. "I'm pulling you off the case."

"I've always been able to take care of myself."

"But you shouldn't have to. If you are no longer consulting for the department, then I believe this person will leave you alone and turn his attention elsewhere. It's strange to me that he's fixated on you."

"Maybe he sees me as the weakest link."

Mom pressed her lips together. "Hmm. Perhaps."

Nancy had never seen her mother look so conflicted. What was really going on? "I want to help find this person." More importantly, she didn't want anyone else to get hurt because of her. If she stopped investigating and the perp turned his attention to her mom or Carter, she would never forgive herself.

"I don't want to argue about this, Nancy."

"Then let me do the job." Something about this conversation seemed off. "Who is putting me on the sidelines? My mom or the sheriff?"

Surprise filled her mother's eyes before she chuckled. "You are most assuredly my daughter, first and foremost." Mom stood and paced to the front window then back. She sighed. "Fine, you can continue, but you're not to do any investigating on your own. Period. I mean it, Nancy. If I hear you were questioning anyone or talking to shopkeepers about surveillance...anything at all, you're done. Got it?"

"Yes, Ma'am. I promise, but how will I maintain my cover if I don't sleuth on my own? If I'm always with a deputy, everyone will suspect I'm working for you." Nancy knew she had her mom in a tough spot. She'd have to admit she was thinking like a mother, not the sheriff.

Her mom narrowed her eyes. "You're a smart woman, figure it out." She stood. "I'm going to bed." She left the room, and a short time later Nancy heard the bedroom door click closed.

She grabbed her smart phone and shot off a text to Carter. "Need to talk." What her mom was demanding was impossible. She couldn't openly work with Carter. She might as well admit defeat, because she was officially off the case if she ever hoped to consult with anonymity for the sheriff's department again.

A moment later her phone rang. "Hi, Carter. Thanks

for calling so fast."

"You said you needed to talk. Is everything okay?"

"No."

"What's wrong?"

"Mom essentially pulled me off the case unless I work with you. She's put me in an impossible situation. I gave my word that I wouldn't work the case without her or you, and I don't see how it's possible. I can only see two ways to make it work, and neither option is ideal. I either quit or find a way to investigate with you and not draw attention to what I'm doing. I simply don't see how working with you is possible without everyone knowing. I'd lose my anonymity as a consultant."

"I'm really sorry. I guess it'd be best if you step away from the investigation."

The disappointment in his voice surprised her. He meant what he said. "Thanks. I'm sorry too, but I'm afraid you will now become this person's target."

"Did something happen? I'm surprised by this turn of events."

"Yes, someone followed me tonight. He tailgated me close enough that had someone been sitting on the hood they could have rested their feet on my trunk."

Silence.

"Hello. Carter, are you still there?" She checked the screen to see if the call dropped.

"I'm here. Tonight as you pulled away, I heard footsteps and then a car door shut. Not that it is so unusual, but I couldn't see anyone. Now that I think about it, that is unusual. I wish I'd pursued the sound."

"No, you did the right thing. You had Maddie and Gavin to take care of. I'm fine, other than being off the case. I'm sorry I let everyone down."

"You didn't let anyone down. We all, your mother included, underestimated whoever is doing this and that's our fault not yours. Tomorrow is my day off. Can you get away for lunch?"

"Sure. Why?"

"Thought we could grab a bite and discuss an idea I have."

"We aren't working together anymore, Carter. You don't have to talk to me now."

He chuckled. "I'm aware of that, Miss Daley. As it happens, I enjoy your company and would like to have lunch with you."

"Oh. Well then, yes. Shoot me a text when you're free."

"Will do. Stay safe."

"You too." She ended the call and did a happy dance.

"What on earth!" Her mother stood in the entryway of the hall that connected the bedrooms to the living area.

Nancy froze. "I thought you went to bed."

"Apparently so." She laughed "Who were you talking to?"

"Carter."

Mom's brow rose. "You said there was nothing between the two of you. Is there something I should know?"

"Nope." She breezed past her. "See you in the morning." She waited until she was out of sight then did a fist pump—Carter had asked her out!

# Chapter Thirteen

"YOU WANT TO WHAT?" NANCY LOOKED at Carter from across the table at Roaster's Coffee, like he had two heads.

"Pretend we're seeing each other." He couldn't tell if she was offended by his suggestion or surprised.

"Why?"

He kept his voice hushed. "So you can continue with the case. I think you're closer than you realize to figuring out who's behind the thefts and that's why you're being threatened. If word gets out that we're dating, then being with me won't stir up any suspicion that you're still investigating. The thing is, you can't tell anyone the truth."

"But I can't lie."

"Normally I would support that motto, but in this case, your life might depend on our ruse. Plus it's not really a lie if we are undercover. What do you say?" He reached across the table for her hand. He knew she couldn't resist a mystery, much less helping someone in need. Not knowing who was behind the missing license plates would eat at her, so he may as well begin their ruse now.

Nancy stared at his hand covering hers. "I didn't say yes."

He grinned at the annoyance in her voice. "But you will."

"Sweet junipers, you're confident." She pulled her

hand from his grasp and crossed her arms. "I need to think about this."

He frowned, placing his hand in his lap. *Sweet junipers?* Why did that sound so familiar? He'd heard her say it before but couldn't shake that it was more than that. He motioned to the half-eaten sandwich on the plate in front of her. "You going to eat that?"

"No. I can get it bagged to go, or if you're still hungry, you can have it."

"No thanks."

She stood with her plate in hand. "Be right back."

He watched her carry her plate to the counter where she spoke to Pepper White, the shop owner. Pepper spoke animatedly. She shook her head, causing her latte-colored ponytail to swing. The petite brunette was a firecracker, and he could see why the two women were friends—they balanced each other out.

Pepper nodded his direction. Uh-oh. It looked like he got caught watching them. He quickly averted his gaze and focused on the other customers. Business was slow since they'd made it a late lunch. Two women sat at a center table, each with a Bible open in front of them. Several men, who looked to be in a business meeting, occupied another table. None of them paid attention to Nancy or anyone else.

Nancy strolled back to the table holding a brown paper bag. "You ready to go?"

He stood. "I'll walk you back to the library."

"That's not necessary."

"I'm well aware." He shook his head. Nancy had an independent streak that would put a toddler to shame. He opened the door for her. "After you."

"Thanks." She stayed by his side as they walked

toward the library. "I decided to take you up on your idea."

His stomach leapt. "I thought you were against it."

She looped her arm through his. "Pepper saw you take my hand, and she was so excited, I didn't have the heart to tell her it wasn't what she thought." She shrugged. "Looks like you're stuck with me. At least until we can figure this out." She shot him a tentative smile. "The offer still good?"

"Yep. My word is good. I work tomorrow but can stop in at the library at some point. The more people who see us together the more believable it will be to whomever is watching you." Plus, he hoped to keep an eye out for anyone paying special attention to Nancy, so he could turn the tables on him. He'd follow that person, catch him in the act of stealing, and end all of this.

"I figured that about you. Your word is important to you. You're an idealist."

He'd never thought of himself that way, but maybe she was right. "Thanks—I think." He wasn't sure how to feel about her assessment of his personality.

Nancy greeted several people as they strolled arm in arm to the library. "Will you walk inside with me?"

"Of course. But why?"

"I've been getting the creeps at work. I feel like I'm being watched there. If someone is watching me, I want him—or her—to see you."

Which begged the question as to why she'd originally turned down his escort. "Anything else I should know?"

"I don't think so." She tapped her chin as if contemplating. "We should get to know one another though, so we can pull off this ruse effectively. I believe in immersing myself in my work."

He chuckled. "So I'm work, huh?"

Her face turned a shade of light pink. "That didn't sound good did it? Sorry. I only meant—"

"Relax, Nancy. We're fine." That was, except for the niggling in the back of his mind. He'd figure that out later. He opened the door for her.

"Thanks." She disengaged her arm from his and breezed inside. "What genre do you like to read?"

"I'm not much of a reader, but when I do read, I lean toward the classics like Hemmingway's *Old Man and the Sea.*"

"Okay. The classics are over there." She pointed.

"Thanks." He hadn't planned to check out any books, but it was a good cover for scoping out who might be watching Nancy. In fact, he might take up visiting the library on a regular basis.

He grabbed a book off the shelf not paying attention to what it was, then found a seat that gave him a clear view of the entire library, including the hall the led to the backdoor. If someone was watching Nancy he'd see him.

Nancy hadn't pegged Carter for a reader of the classics. Somehow, she'd imagined he would be a thriller kind of guy. Then again, maybe he was. It wasn't like the classics didn't have thrillers, they simply weren't categorized that way.

On her computer, she pulled up the spreadsheet with this year's budget. Tara would take care of anyone who needed to check out. A few minutes later a commotion drew Nancy from her work. She looked around for the source of the noise—a few teenaged boys were horsing around in the stacks. She stood and headed their way.

"Excuse me." Nancy used her firm voice. "Shouldn't you be in school?"

Four pairs of eyes turned her way. One of the boys shook his head. "It was a half-day."

"Oh. Well, please keep the noise down or take it outside." She raised her chin slightly, waiting for a response. She recognized the teens from around town but didn't personally know any of them. Was the tall guy Zander? It sure looked like him, but something was different about him, so she wasn't sure.

"Sorry." One of the other boys nudged his buddy.

"Ah...yeah...sorry. We'll keep it down."

"Thanks." She turned and spotted Carter standing at the end of the stacks.

"Everything okay?" He spoke softly as she passed him.

"Yes. Thanks." She sensed his presence beside her but couldn't see him since he was standing just outside her peripheral vision. She turned to confirm her suspicion and grinned. "Did you find a book you'd like to check out?"

He held one up. "I need a library card."

"As it happens, I know the person in charge, and she can help with that." With a flick of her hair, she strutted to her desk and sat. Okay, so she was flirting, but shouldn't she if they were supposed to be dating? If she didn't, people would wonder. She intended to hold up her end of the plan.

A lazy grin covered Carter's face as he pulled out his driver's license and handed it over.

"Thanks." She entered his info, assigned him a card, then handed it back, along with his license. "Guard that card with your life. It's quite valuable."

He raised a brow. "Why's that?"

"That's your key to worlds unknown, adventure, and information." She paused and leaned toward him for effect. "Plus, it will cost you to replace it. Only the first one is free."

He nodded, and she could tell he was fighting laugher. He slipped the card into his wallet. "Aside from my I.D., I believe this is the most valuable item in my wallet." He grasped the book with his other hand as he stuffed his wallet into his pocket. "Do you mind if I stop by your place tonight?"

"Not at all. I walk with Anna Plum right after I get off, but I'll be free after that."

"Great. I'll see you." He nodded toward the stacks. "You might want to check on those boys. They're too quiet."

Her eyes widened. He was right. She charged toward the stacks and stopped when she got to where they'd been horsing around. Two of the boys sat on the floor, each holding a book. "Where are your friends?"

"They left," the same boy that had apologized earlier motioned toward the exit. The tall teen was no longer there.

"Oh. Okay." She turned and headed to her desk. How had she not seen them leave? She'd been distracted by Carter. A smile touched her lips. At first, she'd been disappointed that he had asked her out only to suggest they pretend to date, but the more she thought about his idea the more she saw the wisdom in it. Not only would she still be able to work the case without drawing suspicion, but he'd be around more to keep an eye out for who might be paying too much attention to her.

The hair on the back of her neck stood up. She stilled, listening for anything out of the norm—nothing. The overhead lights buzzed, and a low murmur of voices filled the air. She sat and casually looked around. Something brushed against her foot. She looked down, screamed and leapt to the top of her desk.

Tara raced toward her. "What's wrong?" Concern filled her face.

"Call 911. There's a snake under my desk." Her heart hammered. What should she do? The only thing she knew about snakes was that she hated them.

Tara talked to dispatch and reported the snake. She pulled the phone away from her face. "They're on the way. She wants to know if anyone is in danger."

"How am I supposed to know?" She looked down. "It's huge." Her throat thickened.

Tara leaned over the desk, gasped, then backed away. "It's a python. Someone's pet must have escaped."

"How did it get into the library? I think I would have noticed a huge snake slithering in."

"I don't know, but how about you get off the desk. Very slowly though. You don't want to spook it."

"Like it spooked me?" she asked sardonically. Nancy jumped down to the safe side of the desk. Her entire body shook.

A short time later, the library door swooshed open, and Lyle rushed in, followed by Animal Control. "You okay, Nancy?"

"Other than almost having a heart attack. Yes. Tara thinks it's a python under my desk."

Lyle looked down. "Good thing it's solid on this

side." He shivered like he had the heebie-jeebies. "You got this?" he asked Ben from Animal Control.

Ben leaned over the top and peered down. "Yeah. He looks like he's been fed recently."

Nancy knew enough about snakes to know that was a good thing. "I'll get everyone out of here."

Tara rested a hand on her arm. "Everyone tore out of here not long after you screamed and announced there was a snake under your desk."

"Well, at least you stayed to help."

"My sister has a pet snake. Not as big as that fellow, but generally they won't hurt you."

In a matter of minutes, Ben had the snake contained and out the door.

Lyle shook his head. "This is getting ridiculous. Have you considered going out of town for an extended vacation?"

"No. I'm sure the snake was a harmless prank."

Lyle sighed. "Nancy, prank or not, that was not harmless. You could have been hurt." He rested a hand on her shoulder. "How about you close early. Take the rest of the day off."

"I can't. We had to close the other day because of the smoke bomb. I won't shut down again."

"I don't mind staying and closing up," Tara said. "I think it's a good idea for you to take some personal time. Maybe go spend time with that new boyfriend of yours."

*New boyfriend?* Right, Carter. Her assistant was more observant than she'd realized. Too bad she hadn't spotted the prankster. But wait . . . the surveillance cameras would have, and she could access them from her laptop at home. "I'm going to take you up on that,

Tara. Thanks." She grabbed her purse and left without a backward glance.

Lyle strode beside her. "What are you up to? And what boyfriend?"

"What makes you think I'm up to anything?"

"Evading questions, I see. I've known you most of your life, Nancy. You're up to something."

"Nothing dangerous, so don't worry."

"Why doesn't that make me feel any better?" Lyle headed toward his patrol car.

Nancy went straight home and shot off a text to Carter.

"Had an incident at the library. I'm at home. Can you come over sooner than later?"

Her phone rang. "Hi, Carter."

"What happened?" Concern filled his voice.

She brought him up to speed as she booted up her laptop. "I'm going to run through the surveillance footage. There's no way someone got into the library with a snake that size without being recorded."

Silence greeted her when she stopped talking. "Carter? You still there?" She checked the screen. The call had dropped. Oh well, he'd call back if he could. She sat on the couch and pulled up the footage from the library. Her doorbell pealed. Her stomach knotted. Setting her computer aside she stood and quietly approached the door. She wasn't expecting company.

# Chapter Fourteen

"NANCY, IT'S CARTER," HE SAID FROM outside her front door.

She flung it open. "What are you doing here?"

"I headed your way as soon as you told me what happened. I lost the connection when it went to Bluetooth, and figured I'd catch what I missed when I got here. May I come in?"

She stepped back. "Of course. Sorry." She strode to the couch and sat. "I just pulled up the security camera recording from outside the library for today."

"Good. Fill me in on what I missed when my phone cut out."

She started from the beginning since she had no idea when she'd lost him. "I can't believe no one noticed someone walking into the library with a snake."

"You're assuming someone walked in with the snake during operating hours. What if the snake was already there, and it only needed to be set free?"

She shot him a startled look. "I don't see how that's possible." She returned her focus to the computer. "Look, there are the teen boys I talked to." She peered closer at them. "They don't have anything with them." She sighed. "I thought for sure they were the pranksters."

"I had hoped they were." He frowned.

They finished watching and saw nothing. "I'm beginning to think there's a blind spot in my surveillance cameras."

"Maybe. Can you go back to yesterday's recording? I'd like to see if anything happened after hours. That snake didn't slither into the library on its own. Someone had to have smuggled it inside at some point. It might have been there for days undetected."

Nancy shivered. "Eww. I hope not! The idea makes my skin crawl. I don't think it's been there too long since Ben said it appeared to have been recently fed." She clicked the computer mouse, and within seconds had yesterday's footage running on the screen. She pointed. "Who's that?" A person wearing dark clothing with a hood obstructing their face came into view. He or she pushed a baby buggy with a canopy up, effectively blocking the view of the interior.

"It's impossible to tell, but it looks an awful lot like the person who stole the plate off that truck. The size appears to be about the same."

"What do you think he's up to?" The person walked out of the camera's view.

"I don't know, but my gut tells me there's no child inside that buggy."

Nancy closed the laptop and stood. "Let's assume you're right. The buggy looks like one of those heavy-duty ones, so it could easily hold the weight of a hundred pound snake."

"Agreed." He grinned.

"Why are you smiling?" She didn't see anything to smile about.

"We have another clue."

What was he talking about? She stilled and thought. "Oh!" Assuming the snake person was the license plate thief, they now knew said person owned or at least had access to a snake and a buggy. "But how does one go about tracking down the owner of the snake?"

"We let Ben at Animal Control know we want to talk with whomever shows up to claim the snake. I have a few other ideas I'll pursue as well."

"Of course. I should've thought of that." Some sleuth she was. She plopped down beside Carter and crossed her arms. "I figured if I wasn't investigating, whoever was behind all of this would leave me alone." She tilted her head toward him. "Wishful thinking. I guess I should've known better."

"Maybe seeing you with me makes him think you're still on the case. It was only last night you were pulled off the investigation."

"I suppose. But if that's true, then pretending to be dating isn't going to help unless we make everyone believe we are a solid couple, and that's the only reason we're together."

His eyes widened. "You sure you want to do that? It's one thing to be dating, but being an official couple takes things to a different level."

She sucked in her bottom lip and nodded. What should she do? She wasn't a wimp, but having to look over her shoulder at every turn and worry about what could happen next, slowed her down. If the perp believed they were a couple and spending time together because they were in love, surely things would settle down. She nodded. "I don't think we have a choice. We have to stop this person before someone gets hurt."

A perplexed expression rested on his face.

Her stomach knotted. "If you don't want to do this, I'll understand." He was new to town and probably didn't want to attach himself to her in that way. People would forever associate them together.

"That's not it. I'm thinking about Gavin. I realize this was my idea in the beginning, but I hadn't considered my nephew."

She nodded. His nephew had to be a part of the equation. The two of them were a family, and Carter's actions had a direct impact on Gavin. "Okay. Let me know what he says. Will you tell him the truth?"

"Yes. I have to. We have a rule in our house. No matter what, we don't lie to each other."

She winced. They'd be lying to the whole town. This was a bad idea. "You know what, forget it. I don't like the idea after all."

"Why?"

Should she tell him her deepest regret? It surprised her she'd even consider it. After all it was her deepest, darkest secret, and it wasn't all that long ago she couldn't stand him. He'd grown on her though, and she really liked him now. Clearly he was trustworthy if her suggestion made him so uncomfortable.

"Nancy?"

Her gaze landed on his. She let out a breath. "Sorry. When I was a kid I told a whopper of a lie that I deeply regretted. It didn't turn out all bad though, since after that my mom decided it was time we started attending church."

"Are you a Christian?"

She nodded. "Are you?" Based on everything she'd witnessed about Carter, she knew he was.

"I am."

"Good." Okay, now they were only speaking in one and two-word sentences. That couldn't be a positive sign. She cleared her throat. "So now what?"

"Now I hang out here until you go for your walk with Anna. I don't want you to be alone."

Her palms began to sweat. "I can take care of myself."

"So I've been told. But I'd feel a lot better sticking by your side until we catch this person. I can make a few phone calls to nearby reptile veterinarians to see if they've treated a python while I wait. If there's time, I'll also check with all the pet stores within a fifty-mile radius. My time here won't be wasted."

She nodded. To be honest, the idea of him being here for the next hour was kind of nice. "I could help."

"Sure. If you want to call the pet stores, I'll start with the reptile veterinarians."

Carter hung up with the last exotic animal vet he could find listed online—a dead end. He watched Nancy pace in her kitchen as she spoke to someone at a pet store. She'd come up empty too.

He had to be missing something. He looked down at his notes. Could Nancy be the key to solving this case? Whoever was harassing Nancy had clearly fixated on her. He looked up and caught her watching him. He raised a brow. "Something on your mind?"

"Too much." She moved into the living room and sat beside him.

"Yeah. Me too. I can't help but wonder if you know the perpetrator."

"I know, you mentioned much the same before. Everyone who knows me knows I hate snakes. They also know fire is one of my biggest fears."

He frowned. "I didn't know those things about you."

"You do now, but you're my most recent acquaintance."

He nodded. He didn't like where his thoughts were going, but he had to pursue them. "We looked into anyone who might have been put away as a result of your input—it was a dead end. That likely means someone here in town that you associate with on a personal level is doing this."

Her shoulders slumped forward slightly. "I know. It really hurts. What did I do to make someone hate me enough to do this?"

"Hey." He reached for her hand, waiting for her to look at him. Pain filled her pretty eyes. "This isn't on you, Nancy. I haven't known you very long, but I can say without a doubt, you would never do anything to harm another person intentionally. Whoever is behind this has issues."

Her eyes watered, and she blinked rapidly. "That's very sweet of you. It doesn't change anything, but I'm touched. Thank you." She leaned toward him and placed a kiss on his cheek.

A jolt shot through him.

The doorbell pealed.

Nancy jumped up. "That must be Anna."

He stood. "How about you get changed? I'll let her in." Plus, if it wasn't Anna but instead someone up to no good, he wanted Nancy safely out of sight.

"Good idea." She bolted from the room.

He pulled open the door, immediately recognizing the auburn-haired woman who stood on the other side wearing leggings and a long green shirt. He'd made a point of looking up all of Nancy's friends online so he'd know them by sight. "Nancy's changing. Would you like to come in?"

"Sure. You're the new deputy."

"That's right."

She held out her hand. "It's nice to finally meet you. I have your nephew in my English class." She stepped inside but didn't move beyond the entryway. "He's smart and he's doing a great job with the book club."

"I'm happy to hear that. He's a good kid. Not perfect, but..."

She laughed. "I haven't met a perfect teen yet, and I've been teaching for fifteen years." She chuckled.

Nancy rushed into the room. "Sorry for making you wait. We were talking and lost track of time."

"No problem." Curiosity filled her eyes. "You ready?"

"Yes." Nancy grabbed a plastic key chain and slipped it over her wrist, wearing it like a bracelet. She turned to Carter. "Call me when you've made a decision one way or the other."

*A decision?* Oh right, about them presenting themselves as a serious couple. "Will do. It was great to meet you, Anna. I'm sure we'll run into each other sooner or later."

"That's a given in this town." She turned and walked outside.

Nancy motioned him ahead of her then she locked up. At least she was being careful now.

# Chapter Fifteen

NANCY PUMPED HER ARMS AS SHE strode beside Anna and her hyper dog, Freddy. She'd begun to look forward to this time every afternoon with her neighbor. They'd become good friends—who would have guessed? "I suppose you're going to hear about this sooner or later, so I might as well tell you. That way you can set the story straight in the event the details get twisted."

Anna tilted her head toward Nancy. "This wouldn't have anything to do with the deputy in your living room would it?"

"Indirectly, yes. A python was discovered in the library today—under my desk."

"You're kidding!"

"I wish."

"You poor thing. I know how afraid you are of snakes. Any idea how it got there?"

"None." How long would it take for Anna to connect the dots? Sooner or later the townspeople would start to wonder about all the things happening at the library.

"Are you in danger? Is that why a cop was at your house?"

"It's possible." This would be a perfect time to set the groundwork for their ruse. But she hated deceiving anyone, much less Anna.

"What is 'it's possible' supposed to mean?"

Anna jumped when a car beeped its horn in passing. The driver waved. "Was that Gloria?"

"I think so. She must have another new car. Back to what we were talking about."

Nancy blew out a long breath that steamed in the rapidly cooling late afternoon air. What could she say to satisfy her friend without being untruthful? "Carter and I are testing the waters."

"So you are dating?"

"We have gone out."

Anna squealed like a schoolgirl. "I'm so happy for you. Honestly, I wasn't sure you'd ever give a man a chance since you've shied away from relationships for so long. I can tell he's a good guy."

Nancy felt a little bad because Anna was truly happy for her, and in the end Nancy would disappoint her. "Well, we aren't serious or anything like that, but I do like him." At least that was the truth. Carter was everything she'd want in a husband if she ever chose to marry—a Christian, honest, hardworking, a family man, moral, and surprisingly nice, considering their first few encounters.

Anna's pace slowed. "We've known each other a long time, Nancy."

"Yes?" Where was she going with this?

"I feel like something's off. What aren't you saying?"

If she couldn't trust Anna there was no one she could trust. She looked around to see if there was anyone walking nearby or people out in their yards. It appeared they were alone. Nancy kept her voice low. "What I'm going to tell you needs to stay between us. No one can know. Can you keep a secret? My life could depend on it."

Wide-eyed, Anna nodded.

Nancy filled her in on what had been happening,

leaving out anything that could compromise their case and ending with she was waiting to hear from Carter about their ruse since he had his nephew to consider.

Anna stopped walking and faced her. "Wow. I had no idea all of this was going on. And people say you can't pee in this town without someone knowing."

Nancy chuckled. "Well, that's probably not true." She sobered. "Now that you know our secret what do you think? Are we doing the right thing?"

Anna's lips flattened as she pressed them together. Freddy barked and jumped up. She bent down and cuddled the dog to her chest. "I'm not God or your moral compass. I think you should first pray about this situation and then go from there. As your friend, I hope things work out for the two of you. You make a cute couple. You have chemistry."

"Really?" She liked Carter, but she hadn't noticed anything special between them. Maybe she needed to take a break from thinking about her current mystery and pay more attention to the people around her.

"Absolutely. As far as your safety goes, I'll start carrying my pepper spray when we walk. Plus Freddy here would take a piece out of anyone who tried to harm either of us."

Nancy grinned. "Aww, Freddy. You'd really do that for me?" She reached over and scratched his back. The cutie had wrapped his paws around Anna's neck like a child would. She shook her head. "Your dog looks human—aside from the mass of white fluff, that is."

"Yeah, this guy likes to hang on." She pulled him away from her and looked into his face. "But it's time you walked." She set him down. "It's getting dark. We should head back."

"You're right." A weight that Nancy hadn't realized she carried had been lifted. Having someone to share her secrets helped ease her stress more than she dreamed possible. Would Carter be upset that she'd told Anna? If so, she'd simply assure him her neighbor was trustworthy, and she would never try and harm anyone.

"I kind of envy you."

Nancy shot a look in Anna's direction. "Why?"

"Your life is filled with excitement. And you have the attention of a man that half of the single women in town would kill for. If he were a little older I might even be jealous of his obvious interest in you—and don't tell me it's all an act. I don't buy it."

"You're open to finding love again? I thought you were content to be single."

"I am content, but there's a part of me that yearns to be loved." She shrugged. "At least I have Freddy."

Nancy smiled and nodded. "But you don't need a man to live a happy and fulfilled life."

"Of course not. But I sure would enjoy cuddling by a fire and having a husband to fall asleep talking to. It'd be nice to have someone to share my life's journey with. Don't get me wrong, I'm happy and fulfilled. But the idea of a good man who loves me unconditionally—"

"Is too good to be true. Only God loves that way."

"Perhaps...perhaps not."

Nancy shook her head. "I don't believe that we are capable of unconditional love." Humans didn't love no matter what happened. Her own father had stopped loving her, otherwise he would still be in her life. If a dad could do that, how could anyone believe people were capable of loving, no matter what?

"You might be right. Only the Lord is perfect. We all

have our faults. But I pray if I ever find a man he will love me in spite of my imperfections."

"Amen!" Nancy stopped at the bottom of her driveway noting her mom wasn't home like she'd expected. "You want to come in for a glass of water?"

A knowing look filled Anna's eyes. "Sure. What about Freddy?"

Nancy waved a hand. "So long as he's housetrained he's welcome."

Anna wrinkled her nose. "To be safe, I'll run him home real quick. Be right back."

Nancy killed time in the yard, pulling weeds while she waited. She wasn't afraid to go inside alone, but unease gripped her. Was someone watching her?

The doorbell pealed at Carter's house. He headed toward the door since Gavin was in his bedroom doing homework. Had he invited Maddie over to study again? Carter pulled open the door. Surprised jolted him. "Hi, Lilly. What brings you by?"

His real estate agent smiled. "I like to pop in on my buyers to see how things are going. I realize you are renting until escrow closes but wanted to check in anyway."

"Wow, that's amazing customer service." Cool air rushed inside. "Would you like to come in?"

"Sure. Thanks, but only for a minute."

He opened the door wider and stepped aside for her.

She stopped in the entryway. "How is everything?"

"Fine. The house hasn't dumped any surprises on us, so that's a plus. I'm thankful Nancy gave me your number."

Lilly's eyes lit. "Me too." She held out her business card. "I love referrals."

"Sure." He pocketed the card.

"How are you settling into town?"

"Great. Have you heard otherwise?" He raised a teasing brow.

Her face flushed. "No. The opposite. From what I hear, you snagged Nancy's attention. That's quite an accomplishment considering she's shunned men for as long as I can remember."

He crossed his arms. Where was this going? "Really? I never got a man-hater vibe from her."

"I didn't mean it that way. What I meant was that I've never known her to date. It's not like men aren't interested either."

"O-kay." He drew the word out. "Why are we talking about Nancy?"

She laughed. "Sorry, I ramble when I'm nervous."

"I make you nervous?" A lot of people were intimidated by law enforcement, but he hadn't sensed that from Lilly.

"Not really. I guess I'm always nervous when I check in on my clients. I want everything to be perfect for them." She shrugged. "What can I say, I have anxiety about silly things."

"Oh. I see. You have no need for concern here. The house is great. I appreciate you stopping by to check."

"Wonderful. I'm happy to hear it." She flashed a perfect smile. "I'll see you at closing, Carter."

He went back into his house, perplexed by her concern, but who was he to judge. It seemed everyone had quirks. He strode up the stairs to Gavin's room and stood in the doorway. "I need to run something by you, and I want an honest answer."

A worried look settled on his nephew's face. "That doesn't sound good. Did I do something wrong?"

"Not that I know of. You have something to confess?"

"Nope."

Carter grinned. This parenting thing had its ups and downs, but he was beginning to enjoy it regardless. "First off, I need you to understand what I'm about to tell you is top secret."

Gavin laughed. "Yeah, right."

"Totally serious. Not government top secret, but someone's life might depend on your silence. Can I trust you?"

"Will telling me put me in danger?"

"Good question and no."

"Okay. What's up?"

"Nancy Daley and I need to pretend to be a couple for a while."

"Why?"

"I can't say, but it's really important that everyone believes our story."

He shrugged. "Whatever. Your secret is safe."

"You don't mind?"

"Why should I?"

"I'll be spending more time with her, and she'll be around more."

Gavin shrugged. "She's around a lot anyway. I kind of thought you had a thing for her. I didn't realize it was a performance. You're a pretty good actor, Uncle Carter."

"Thanks?"

His nephew laughed. "That was a compliment. Can

Maddie come over later? We need to choose our next book for the book club. We thought we'd find one online this time."

"Sure. I might invite Nancy too then. Remember the thing about Nancy and me is top secret. Maddie can't know."

"No problem." Gavin grinned then turned his attention back to the book on his desk. Carter sauntered to the living room and parked himself on the couch. It was time to tell Nancy that Operation Fake Out was a go.

# Chapter Sixteen

"MOM, I'M GOING OUT TO DINNER with Carter tonight." Nancy stood in the kitchen as her mother pulled a casserole from the oven. She'd decided to fill her mom in on their ruse. She didn't want her mom to start dreaming about a wedding that wasn't happening.

"I wish you would have said something sooner. I wouldn't have bothered to cook."

"I'm sorry, it was a last-minute thing. Will you be okay on your own?" She was beginning to think her mom was sticking around simply because she enjoyed the company and not to be her protector. If Mom knew what she'd found taped to the library door this morning she probably wouldn't let her out of her sight.

Mom chuckled. "I'll be fine, dear. You go have fun, and when you get home we'll have hot cocoa and you can tell me all about your date. Word around town is the two of you will be engaged by the New Year." She winked.

Nancy shook her head. "I guess people have nothing better to gossip about." It looked like they had fooled everyone—except their plan had backfired. To make matters worse, her heart was beginning to believe their ruse. If only they could catch her stalker. Frustration at their lack of a solid lead had reached a frenzy. They needed a break in this case right away.

"I wish that were true. We've had several burglaries over the past few weeks. I'm beginning to think it's the same person or group."

Nancy slipped into her coat. "No kidding?" Why hadn't Carter said anything? It wasn't like he hadn't had the opportunity, considering they were together practically every day since they decided to move forward with their idea.

"Yes. It's strange. Tipton's always been a place where you can leave your house and car unlocked without worry. Things are sure changing."

Nancy frowned. Was it really that serious? Had big city crime reached its tentacles as far as little Tipton, Oregon? "I'm sorry to hear about that. Do you have any leads?"

"None."

"I hope the case breaks soon. See you in the morning." Mom always went to bed early and was up before the sun. She pulled open the door and gasped. "Carter, I thought we were meeting there."

He shook his head. "Change of plans. Do you mind?"

She shrugged and closed the door behind her. "It's fine, so long as we eat. I'm starving. The library was busy today, and I didn't have time for more than a cup of coffee and a donut." Not that she'd had much of an appetite once she'd spotted the note on the library door.

"Isn't that what you get *before* you open the library during your Friday morning ritual with Pepper?"

"You know about that?" She didn't recall mentioning it, but maybe she had.

He nodded as he held the car door for her.

She settled inside. This felt more like a date than any of their past outings. Could he be feeling what she was? Until tonight when he held the door for her, he'd never given a hint to her that he might actually be interested in her—okay, maybe she was reading too much into his gentlemanly gesture. Ha, she was definitely reading too much into it. His feelings, or lack thereof aside, to the outside world, she was certain, based on her mom's comment, they looked like a couple in love. And that was what was important.

He slid behind the wheel and started the engine. "I have an ulterior motive for picking you up." He glanced her way before returning his attention to the road.

"What is it?" Would this be when he declared his undying love for her? She almost laughed at the ridiculous thought.

"We're headed to a place in the next town over. I got a tip I thought we could check out together."

"Oh." The letter could wait a little longer. Excitement and disappointment swirled through her. Argh, she needed to stop acting like a lovesick teen and focus on the reason they were together—to solve a mystery. "So the tip is credible?"

"I think so, otherwise we wouldn't be pursuing it. The manager at the new storage units in Payton called about suspicious activity and possible stolen goods."

"As in weapons and electronics or license plates?"

"Not license plates."

"Then why am I going? This is a police matter that I'm not involved with."

"Because I'm running with the theory that the same person or persons are involved with both cases. I needed to follow up on this right away, and I didn't want to cancel on you."

Nancy's stomach jolted. He really did want to be with her. Maybe her thoughts earlier weren't so far off base after all. The letter in her purse bothered her more than she cared to admit and needed to be taken seriously, but it would keep until after their date. She didn't want anything to ruin this evening.

"We are being watched so closely in town I figured if we weren't seen together on a Friday night tongues would wag. When we're done investigating we can come back to town and pop in to BLB."

Nancy couldn't summon a response. This yoyo of emotions was taking a toll on her. Carter must not have noticed since he didn't pursue the conversation further. Twenty minutes later they rolled to a stop at a mini storage facility.

"Looks quiet."

"It looks closed to me. Are you sure about this?" Unease settled on her. She wasn't a wimp but didn't look for trouble either.

"The manager said he'd talk with us. Come on."

Nancy met him at the hood of his car. "Where is he?"

Carter nodded toward the office. "There's a light on inside."

She kept pace beside him. Her stomach knotted as Carter pulled open the door to the office.

"Hello?"

A man stepped into the small, but tasteful space from a back room. Clearly the facility was new, from the freshly painted walls to the pristine tile flooring.

Carter held out his hand. "You must be Will. I'm Deputy Malone, and this is my associate Ms. Daley. We spoke on the phone earlier today."

"Right. Thanks for coming." He reached for a set of keys and walked around to their side of the counter. "I only entered the unit because the rent hadn't been paid. I tried contacting the owner several times and even sent a letter. I figured I could sell the stuff."

Carter nodded. "Will you show us the unit?"

"Yep. Follow me." The man led them along the side of the building and stopped at a single garage door. A moment later he had the door up and a light on.

Carter whistled. "Looks like quite a stash of weapons. Have you told anyone else about this?"

"No sir."

"Do you have a picture of the person who's renting the unit?" Why would someone with this kind of arsenal neglect to pay the rent? It didn't make sense. Was the manager's story only an excuse to give him reason to poke around?

The manager shook his head. "Never thought of it."

"I see you have a surveillance camera. Maybe—"

"Nope. It's a dummy camera to deter crime."

Carter blew out a breath. "Okay." He handed the man his card. "If you see the owner, let me know."

"What do I do with the guns?"

"Nothing. Someone will be in touch."

"That's it?"

"For now, yes. We appreciate the call, and again, if you see the owner call me."

The man pulled the door down while muttering something rude.

Nancy cleared her throat and motioned Carter with her eyes toward the car.

Carter nodded and together they walked to his vehicle.

"Why so quiet?" Nancy glanced his way.

"Thinking."

"Is there a jurisdiction issue?"

"Possibly." He sighed. "I'm really sorry about this, but I need to make some calls before we leave."

"It won't keep until tomorrow?" She'd grown up around law enforcement and knew the answer, but the question popped out before she could stop it.

"Afraid not."

An hour later, after Nancy's mom and a deputy showed up to take over, the situation was well in hand so they could leave. It was annoying to have to wait around for law enforcement, and then for Carter to fill everyone in, but she was used to the way things worked and didn't complain despite her growling stomach.

Carter studied Nancy for a brief moment before turning his attention back to the road. "I'm starving. I'm sorry this took so long, I know you said you haven't eaten since this morning."

"Don't worry about it. I'm actually surprised you still want to go out for dinner. You don't mind turning that scene over to my mom and the rest of the team?" Confusion filled Nancy's voice. "This is, after all, your case."

"It's fine. She'll keep me in the loop, and we get to cut out and eat. It sure beats hanging out at that storage unit." He glanced her way as he pulled into a parking spot on Main Street.

"I suppose."

He chuckled and reached for her hand. "I won't lie to you. If I say it's okay, it is." He understood her doubt. But his boss was in charge of the scene now, and she was surprisingly good at what she did for being an elected lawwoman. Then again, from what he'd learned, the sheriff had been just like him once upon a time and was well versed in all aspects of law enforcement.

Nancy glanced down at their linked hands.

Heat crept up his neck. He released her hand.

She swung the door open and got out without waiting for him to get her door. "Where to? Do you still want to go to Best Little Burgers?"

"What are you in the mood for?"

A crash in the alley drew his attention, but he hesitated. He wasn't on duty, and he'd already allowed his job to take over their date. Who was he kidding? Only himself. This date was part of his job—a very pleasant part.

"Sweet juniper, Carter. Aren't you going to see what's going on?" Nancy whispered.

His gut clenched at the memory of why that phrase was so familiar. He studied Nancy's face. Could she be the friend he'd had for the short time they lived in town, all those years ago? "It's probably a cat."

She nudged him toward the alley. "Go check." She kept her voice low.

He clenched his jaw. "Fine, but not because you told me to." Okay, that was immature. The lack of food was affecting his mood for sure. He approached the alley—his senses on alert. He poked his head around the corner unwilling to completely expose himself since the streetlamp behind him would make him an easy target if someone up to no good waited in the alley.

A cat meowed and raced past him.

His heart rate slowed to normal. Funny, he hadn't realized his adrenaline had kicked in. "It was only a cat, like I thought."

Nancy nodded. "Good. You ready to get dinner?"

"Yes." The word slipped out without a thought. He needed to eat, but all he really wanted to do was figure out if the Nancy he knew now could have been his playmate all those years ago—the playmate who had lied about him and got him into all kinds of trouble. He'd heard Nancy's mom had divorced...was it possible she'd returned to her maiden name after her divorce?

Nancy pulled the door open to BLB and hesitated as she looked at him and shrugged. "Is this still where you want to eat?"

"Sure." It didn't matter where they ate. He followed her up the stairs to the second story restaurant and to a table by a window. Should he tell her who he was? Obviously, she didn't remember him. There was no reason why she should. She hadn't valued their friendship the way he had, or she never would have told her mom that he'd shoplifted candy all those years ago when they were kids—he was innocent, but no one would believe him.

"Earth to Carter. Come in."

He shook away his thoughts. "What were you saying?"

"I asked what you were going to order. Are you okay? You look like you might be coming down with something."

"I'm not sick." At least not the kind of sick she was talking about, but he needed air. "On second thought, I'm not feeling up to sitting here. Do you mind getting your meal to go and then I'll take you home?"

"If you're not eating, I won't either. My mom made dinner." She stood, giving him a curious look. "I hope you're not getting the flu."

"Me too." He might not have the flu, but he felt knocked off his feet just the same. He never dreamed Nancy was his long-ago playmate, but now that he knew he couldn't imagine how he'd not realized it. Yes, she looked and sounded different, but her eyes and smile were still the same as when they were first graders.

Nancy slipped her hand around his arm. "Would you like me to drive?"

"Depends. Do you consider this an emergency?"

She laughed. "I promise to drive the speed limit."

"Actually, I'll drive."

"You sure?" Concern filled her voice.

"Positive." He opened her car door and waited for her to get in, then took a bracing breath before getting behind the wheel. It wouldn't do any good to bring up the past. They were kids, and kids did and said stupid things. Except what she did changed the course of his life. She was the reason he'd gone into law enforcement. That wasn't a bad thing, but his experience here as a child had made a huge impact on his life. He pulled out and headed toward Nancy's.

"Please don't be mad."

His grip tightened on the steering wheel. "What would I be mad about?"

"I haven't been as forthright as I should be."

Did she know who he was? "What are you talking about?"

She opened her purse and pulled out a zipped bag with a piece of paper inside. "I found this taped to the library door this morning."

His stomach lurched. "Another threat?"

"Unfortunately. I know I should've shown you this first thing, and I know my timing stinks, but my conscience won't let me put it off any longer."

He pulled over to the side of the road so he could look at her. "Why are you telling me this now?"

"I had hoped to have a nice time tonight. I didn't want to spoil our date." She added air quotes around the word date. "But since our evening is officially over..."

"You decided to top it off with a cherry."

She grimaced.

"May I see the letter?"

She handed it to him. Using the flashlight on his phone he read the letter.

STAY AWAY FROM THE COP IF YOU KNOW WHAT'S GOOD FOR YOU.

His stomach knotted. "This sounds personal."

She took a breath and let it out slowly. "I was afraid of that too. What should we do?"

# Chapter Seventeen

"GOOD AFTERNOON, MADDIE." NANCY WALKED OVER to the reading nook where the teen sat. "Happy Hump Day."

The girl raised her brows. "Hi."

"How's the book club going?"

"Great. Another person joined this week." Maddie grinned.

Nancy leaned on the arm of a chair. "I knew you'd make a good leader. How are things going with Gavin? Is he still helping out?"

Maddie's face blossomed a pretty shade of pink. "He is. I'm glad Miss Plum asked us to lead the group together. It's a lot of fun having a partner. Besides that he's a great friend."

"Miss Plum is a smart lady." Nancy nodded. She'd come to the same conclusion regarding the boy's uncle. But they were staying away from one another after the last note. He didn't want to put her in danger, and at this point she was taking the threats seriously.

"I agree." She glanced at the book in her lap then quickly back at Nancy.

"I'll leave you to your reading. I just wanted to say hi and see how things were going."

"Thanks." Maddie offered a genuine smile. It seemed things were looking up for the teen. Now that Nancy thought about it, the pranks had stopped. Could it be the girl had been bored?

Nancy strolled back to her desk being sure to note

where each of the patrons were among the stacks. By her count there were ten visitors in the library.

Ben from Animal Control strolled in. He ambled over to the travel section. What was the man up to? The only other time she'd seen him here was the day he'd caught the snake. Tara shelved books on shelves, two stacks over from Ben.

Ben caught her attention and motioned with his eyes toward the hall. Nancy glanced around to see if anyone looked ready to check out. Everyone appeared engrossed in what they were doing. She stood and wandered toward the hall then pretended to be busy reading a flyer on the bulletin board. A moment later she sensed someone behind her.

"Don't turn," Ben said. "There's been a development."

"What are you talking about," she whispered. "And why can't I turn around?"

"I found the owner of the snake. Meet me in the park after the library closes."

"Why can't you talk now?"

Silence.

"Ben?" She turned. He was gone. How odd. She should let Carter know about the development. He'd want to be there too. On second thought, that would be a bad idea. They were avoiding one another as much as possible to appease whoever had sent the notes.

Nancy meandered to her desk and got back to work. She glanced at the clock for the third time in ten minutes and sighed. Thankfully, it was Wednesday, and the library closed early or she'd probably go nuts waiting for the last hour to creep by.

At four o'clock she walked out with Tara by her side.

"See you tomorrow."

"You seem in a hurry. Are you doing something fun tonight?"

"I wish. I have a meeting to get to."

Tara nodded then turned and headed in the opposite direction of the park.

Nancy spied Lyle across the street in his cruiser. "I wonder what he's up to." She walked over to him. "Good afternoon."

"Hi, Nancy. Everything okay?"

She nodded. "Looks like Ben with Animal Control has a lead on the owner of that snake."

His brows shot up. "Why wasn't I notified?"

She shrugged. "I'm meeting him now. I'd invite you to come along, but he was acting all cloak and dagger. The uniform might put him over the top."

Lyle laughed. "I'll take my chances. Hop in, and I'll give you a ride."

"How are things?" Ever since the last note, her mother had banished her from the courthouse, and she hadn't seen much of the deputies.

"I'm under orders to not talk shop with you. I'm sorry."

Nancy's stomach clenched. Her mom had gone too far this time. "I thought the sheriff trusted me."

He chuckled. "You know she does. But she doesn't want you hurt."

Nancy sighed. "I get that, but it's sure frustrating."

"I know, and I'm sorry." He pulled into a parking spot.

She looked around the park from their vantage point and didn't spot Ben. "How's Deputy Malone doing?"

"He fits in well."

"You know that's not what I meant."

"And you know I can't talk—"

"Yeah, yeah. Look, there's Ben by that stand of trees." She got out. "Thanks for the ride."

"Not so fast. I'm coming too." Lyle opened the door and stepped out.

"But I thought you understood that Ben seemed spooked."

"Which is exactly why I'm joining you. Your mother would have my hide if anything happened to you on my watch."

"Your watch?" She crossed her arms. She and her mother had discussed her use of taxpayer's dollars to keep an eye on Nancy, and they'd both agreed it was a problem. "I thought my mom—"

He raised a hand. "Relax. She told me we're not keeping an eye on you anymore, and I've followed her orders. I happened to be parked across the street from the library working on a report when you stepped outside. I promise it was a complete coincidence."

Her shoulders relaxed. "Okay." She turned toward where Ben was a moment ago. "Oh no. He's gone." Disappointment shot through her. "You don't happen to have his phone number?"

Lyle shook his head. "But I can get it. Hold on a second." He spoke to dispatch, and a minute later, wrote the number on the notepad he carried in his pocket. "Thanks." He punched the number into his cell.

She should be the one making the call, but knew arguing with Lyle was pointless. He was not a man she wanted to cross. Though professional and kind to her, his stature was a little intimidating. He knew his way around the gym, and the girth of his biceps would give even a hardened criminal pause.

The commander frowned as he pocketed his phone. "What's wrong?"

"It went to voicemail."

Alarm shot through Nancy. What if something had happened to Ben? He'd seemed nervous. "Now what?" Would he answer if she called?

"I'll put out a BOLO. I don't have a good feeling about his disappearance."

Nancy nodded. A "Be on the Lookout" was a good idea. With the deputies officially watching for Ben, one of them was sure to find him. She nibbled her bottom lip. But what if they didn't? She did a quick search online for his phone number and came up empty. "Can I have his number?"

He shook his head. "You know I can't give you that." He looked apologetic. "I'll give you a ride back to your car." Lyle opened his vehicle's door.

"No thanks. I'd like to walk."

"You sure? It's kind of cold." He peered up at the cloudy sky.

"Positive. Thanks." She waited for him to pull away then strolled toward to a bench on the edge of the playground. Maybe Ben was still nearby and had only been spooked by Lyle. She zipped her coat and sat. Cold seeped through her slacks. At least the warm and practical boots she'd worn today kept her feet toasty. She stuffed her hands into her pockets and tucked her chin.

Thirty minutes later she stood. Where had Ben gone, and why did seeing a cop with her spook him? She hoofed it back to her car and headed for the courthouse where the Animal Control office was housed. Although she was unofficially banned from the courthouse, her mom would have to understand. Maybe the receptionist could help her locate Ben.

She took the elevator down. As the door slid open she spotted Carter walking through the hall. Though tempted to call out to him, she pressed her lips together. He had made it clear that they needed to stay away from each other. She shook off the sadness brought on by seeing him and not being able to talk to him. She missed him. How had she grown fond of him in such a short time?

He turned at that moment. His gaze met hers. She smiled and waved, but he only nodded. He didn't even look happy to see her. What was up with that? He used to greet her warmly. It's like they'd had a fight and he was mad at her, but they hadn't fought at all.

She turned toward the Animal Control doorway and stepped inside the closet-sized office and faced the lone desk. At least they had an office. She'd heard of some counties where Animal Control was run by the sheriff's department. "Hi, LuAnn."

"Nancy," the middle-aged woman said with a smile. "What brings you down to the basement?"

"I'm looking for Ben. Any idea where he might be?"

"He checked in about an hour ago. Said he wasn't feeling well and was heading home."

"Is that normal?"

She shook her head. "No. He must feel really sick. Is this a personal matter or business that I can help you with?"

"I'm not sure. He stopped by the library earlier and told me he located the owner of the snake."

LuAnn's brow furrowed. "That's the first I've heard of it. Want me to track him down for you?"

"That would be great. When you reach him please give him my number." She grabbed a piece of scratch paper from her purse and wrote out her cell phone number.

"Will do."

Nancy left and went straight for the elevator. Someone strode up, and she glanced at the person beside her—Carter. She followed his lead and remained silent. The doors slid open, and they stepped inside.

The doors closed, and Carter pressed the button for one floor up. "We need to talk."

"Okay. When and where?"

"The state park where we met up before. Fifteen minutes?"

"Sure. That works." She kept her focus on the light above the doors listing the floor levels. The elevator stopped, and the doors opened. She headed out. Something weird was going on, and she aimed to get to the bottom of it one way or another.

Carter strode beside Nancy along the pathway in the park. "Thanks for meeting me here."

"Not a problem. What's going on?"

That was the question of the day. So much had happened, he wasn't sure where to start. "Lyle filled me in on Ben."

Nancy stumbled.

He reached out and caught her arm. "You okay?"

"Yes. It's getting a little dark to see well."

"Let's turn around. Until someone locates Ben you

need to be careful. We believe he knows who is behind this, and if that person thinks he told you, you might be in danger."

"More than I've been all along?"

"Yes. We could be wrong, but I'd rather be safe than sorry." Even though he had been shocked and angry when he realized she was the childhood friend who had accused him of shoplifting—a blatant lie—he was determined to do his job. As long as he was on the case, no one would hurt Nancy.

"Thanks. How do you propose to keep me safe without being with me?"

There was no censure in her voice, only curiosity. "I can't do it alone, that's for sure." He took a breath and let it out slowly. He had hoped it wouldn't come to this, but he didn't know what else to do. "I have a friend. A woman I worked with in L.A. She happens to be in town."

"A girlfriend?"

"No. Just a friend. Jessie has family in Portland so decided to stop in for a couple of days."

"That was nice of her. But I don't see how this relates."

"No one here knows her. She hasn't even been outside my house since she arrived earlier today. I think she could help us." How did he convince Nancy to go with his plan without giving away Jessie's secret?

Nancy's head whipped in his direction. "How and why hasn't she left your house? What aren't you saying?"

He groaned. He knew she'd have questions. She always did. "Jessie is, or rather was, on administrative leave. I can't say more. Her family was asking a lot of questions, and she wanted a place to lie low."

"She's a cop?"

"Yes. A good one. I'd trust her with my life."

"And you want me to trust her with mine." It wasn't a question.

"I do. Look, Nancy. I can only do so much. I've interviewed everyone seen entering the library, which was our best lead. No one raised a flag."

"That's because whoever left the smoke bomb came through the back door. It had a trick lock, which I had fixed after the incident. I told you this."

"I know, but I still wanted to question everyone. The person could have easily entered through the front doors out of a desire to watch your reaction." He stopped at the edge of the path that led to the parking lot.

She faced him. "How are you going to talk your friend into helping us?"

His gut tightened. "I don't know yet."

She sighed. "Fine. Do whatever you think is best, and if she needs a place to stay she's welcome at my place."

"Thank you. There's something unrelated I think you should know."

She shivered.

Cold seeped through his jacket. "Let's go sit in my car." A moment later, he started the engine and set the heater to high. "That day we met in the park, when you were chasing down Anna's dog, wasn't the first time we'd met."

"It wasn't?"

"No. I lived here for a while as a child. You told your mom I shoplifted candy from the store. Shortly after, my dad got a new job in another town and we packed up and left." He shrugged. "My parents never put down deep roots."

She gasped. "That was you? But his name wasn't Carter."

"Everyone called me Junior back then. When I became an adult I started going by my actual name."

Nancy sighed. "You have no idea how horrible I felt about what I did to you. Aside from being older and wiser, I'm not that person anymore. After I fessed up to my mom, she started taking me to church, and it changed my life."

He remembered her mentioning that but hadn't realized he was part of the story. "I'm still trying to wrap my brain around the fact you and my childhood friend are the same person."

"Technically the same, but I'm a very different person now, and I'm so sorry for what I did. I hope you'll forgive me."

Silence filled his car. The Bible commanded him to forgive, and in reality, she'd done him a favor—although at the time he'd been miserable, angry, and confused. He loved being a cop and suspected he wouldn't be one today without Nancy's lie. "I forgive you." A weight lifted off him he hadn't realized was there.

She let out a breath and reached for his hand. "Thank you."

Was she crying? His heart melted, and he pulled her close, wrapping her in his arms.

# Chapter Eighteen

A HEALING BALM WASHED OVER NANCY as she rested her head on Carter's shoulder. She didn't deserve his forgiveness, yet he freely gave it. An image of her dad flashed in her mind. She sat up and scooted to her side of the car, breaking contact with Carter.

"You all right?"

"Yes. I uh...I should get home before my mom worries."

"I'll follow to make sure you get there okay. After I talk with Jessie, I'll let you know what she says."

Nancy popped the door open and got out. "Sounds good." She clicked the remote on her key ring then slid into her car. Dread filled her. She didn't want Carter's friend shadowing her all day at work, and more importantly she wasn't sure what to do with her feelings for Carter. Granted, he hadn't expressed an undying love for her. The hug in his car was probably only him comforting her.

"That had to be it." Her voice sounded loud in the quiet car. She clicked on the radio and pointed her vehicle toward home. Carter's headlights shone in her rearview mirror. Driving straight home, she tried to ignore him. But the pitter-patter in her chest belied her—she was very much aware of the man.

She shook her head. There was no time to think about Carter. Ben was missing, and she could be in someone's sights. Who in this town hated her so much they'd threaten her repeatedly?

She'd thought everyone liked her, but of course that was ridiculous. No one was liked by everyone one hundred percent of the time. Who had she offended? In truth, her life was basic. She opened the library five days a week and spent her entire time there helping people. She went to church, volunteered in the children's program, and had a limited social life. Aside from her work with the sheriff's department, she led a quiet life.

Nancy pulled into her driveway noting her mom's car was missing. Had she worked late? Nancy set the brake then headed inside. She peered out the window from the darkened house to see if Carter still sat behind her parked vehicle, but he was gone. Disappointment struck her. She turned from the window and tugged off her boots then padded to the kitchen to find her chocolate stash. She'd been trying to cut back, but after a day like today, it was a necessity.

Nancy pulled open the drawer and smiled at the sight. Her mom must have stocked her candy drawer. She grabbed a chocolate covered caramel bar then went to the sofa and plopped down. Pulling the wrapper apart, she breathed in deeply of the sweet scent. She could never get enough of that fragrance. Well, maybe she could, but not right now.

Three bites later she wrapped the remainder and set it aside. As much as she loved it, she couldn't over indulge. The front door swung open, and Nancy jumped. Relief washed through her, and she breathed easy. "Hi, Mom."

"Hi yourself. Lyle filled me in on Ben."

Nancy frowned. "Yeah, that's a real mystery. Did

anyone find him?"

"No, and that's what concerns me the most." Mom slid out of her sheriff's jacket and hung it on the hook by the door.

"Are you worried about his safety?"

The rocking chair creaked as her mom sank into it. "I am. He hasn't answered repeated calls. No one seems to know where he is."

"I suppose he could've taken off for the weekend."

"It's possible, but with the Harvest Festival, he should be on duty."

"I can't believe I've completely forgotten about the festival. I always run the cakewalk and spaced out on getting donations. It looks like there won't be one this year." Clearly, she'd been preoccupied.

"Don't worry about the cakewalk. I heard that Anna Plum is running it this year."

"No wonder no one called about it." Anna had become a good friend. She'd have to remember to thank her later. "I need to tell you something."

"That sounds ominous." Mom's brow furrowed.

"Do you remember the boy I was friends with as a kid that I said stole the candy bar?"

She nodded.

"That little boy grew up to be Carter."

"So he finally figured it out and told you, or did you figure it out first? Either way is good. It's about time the truth came out."

Nancy's eyes widened at the implication of her mother's words. "You knew, and you didn't say anything to either of us? How? He doesn't look at all like he did as a boy."

"You're right, but I vetted him before hiring him. His

brother is incarcerated, so I dug a little deeper than I normally would. I put all the pieces together and realized who he was."

"Oh. Why didn't you tell us?"

She shrugged. "The past was a long time ago, and I choose to live in the present." She slapped a hand on her thigh and stood. "You have dinner yet?"

Nancy glanced at the chocolate bar.

Mom chuckled. "Chocolate doesn't count. I'll whip us up a salad and put the chicken I've had marinating all day in the grill pan."

Nancy's stomach growled as she followed her. "He said he forgives me."

"Carter?"

"Mm-hmm." She nodded as she pulled a bowl from the cupboard for the salad.

"Forgiveness is a wonderful gift."

"I agree. Have you forgiven my father for leaving us?" She watched her mom closely.

Mom stilled. She cleared her throat. "That was quite a leap."

"Not really. I think you know I have trust issues because of him leaving us."

"And Carter reminds you of your dad?"

"Not him as a person, but he did come to town shortly after dad left, and it's hard not to think about him when I ruminate about that time in my life."

Mom pulled the grill pan from the cupboard and set it on the stove to heat, then pulled open the fridge and began to stack salad fixings on the counter. "The thing about chewing on the past is that it often will leave a bad taste in your mouth. Take this endive for example. By itself, it's bitter to the taste, but mix it with other greens and add a chopped apple with dressing, and the bitterness is mellowed."

Nancy frowned. "I know there's a point there, but I'm missing it."

Mom grinned as she rinsed the vegetables. "My point is if you focus on the bitter lettuce and don't add all the other good stuff to it you'll get a mouthful of yuck."

"Dad is the mouthful of yuck?"

Mom laughed. "Oh, Nancy. I love you. In plain English, yes, your dad's leaving was a bitter pill to swallow—to use a cliché. Sorry."

Nancy grinned and motioned for her to continue.

"But in retrospect there was a lot of good too. For starters I have you, and I don't have to share you with him. His leaving made me grow as a person, and I hope I'm better for it. Would we have been better off if he'd never left?" She shrugged. "Hard to say. He wasn't a happy man, and there's no telling what our lives would have become had he stuck around."

"So you've forgiven him for leaving you?"

"I have. Mind you, I was angry. Boy was I angry and scared and hurt. But gradually those emotions faded, and I was able to see the good all around me and know that he was only one man. Not *every* man." Mom looked pointedly at her. "Capeesh?"

Nancy nodded. Anna had said much the same. But if they were both telling the truth, why had neither of them married after they were abandoned. She whipped her gaze toward her mom's. "Are you and Dad still married?"

"Goodness, no. He sent me divorce papers six months after he took off. That's when I changed back to my maiden name. Your dad gave up his parental rights, so I changed yours too."

"I didn't know." All the pieces began to make sense now. She'd never understood why her name had changed and was always too afraid to ask—to know.

Mom placed the chicken in the grill pan on the stove. A sizzle ripped through the silence. "Thought I'd cook up a few extras for tomorrow."

"Okay." Nancy didn't care for reheated chicken, but it didn't really matter. She focused on chopping celery.

The doorbell pealed.

"You expecting company?" Mom wiped her hands and strode toward the door.

"I'm not sure. Maybe. Carter has a friend visiting from out of town that needs a place to stay. I said she could stay here."

Mom stopped and turned back to her. "A woman?"

She nodded. "They worked together. She's on leave."

A knowing look filled her mother's eyes as she pulled open the door.

Carter.

A tingle zipped through Nancy.

He stood beside a woman who looked to be nearing thirty. Dark circles lined her eyes. Her bleached blonde hair was pulled back in a ponytail. She didn't look at all like Nancy had imagined. How could this delicate looking woman be a cop? Nancy's mom was made of sturdy-stock, as was she.

Mom moved back. "Come in. Did you eat?"

Carter cleared his throat. "No, but I'm not staying long. This is my friend Jessie."

Nancy eased past her mother and smiled warmly at the woman whose eyes spoke volumes to her comfort level—not good. "I'm Nancy. I hope this isn't a terrible inconvenience."

"It's fine. I planned to be in town for a few days anyway. I might as well stay busy." She offered a smile, but she looked sad. It probably had to do with whatever made her leave L.A., but Nancy wouldn't pry. The woman had clearly been through enough.

Mom closed the door and headed into the kitchen.

Cater stuffed a hand into his jeans pocket. "When I told Jessie what's going on, she agreed you need a bodyguard."

"Do you protect people often?"

"Only in my off time. It seems you could use a little help right now."

Nancy nodded. "Please don't be offended, but you don't look like a cop."

Jessie's features relaxed. "You were right, Carter. I do like her."

Nancy chuckled. "You told her she'd like me?" She couldn't help the surprise in her voice. After all, she hadn't made a good first impression when they'd met. Clearly things had changed.

"Of course." He winked.

Nancy's eye's widened. "Mom and I were preparing dinner. Would you like to join us?" She directed her question to both of them, even though Carter said he wouldn't be staying.

He shook his head. "Thanks, but Gavin's at home. Maddie is coming over, so I need to get back." He turned his head and spoke softly to Jessie.

She nodded then raised a duffle bag. "Is there a place I can store this?"

"Sure. How about you set it off to the side for now. I

need to work out the logistics for tonight." Her mom occupied the only guest room in the house and there was no way her bodyguard was sleeping on the couch. Then again, maybe she'd prefer it.

"Nancy? A word?" Her mom called from the kitchen.

"Have a seat in the living room. I'll be right back."

Jessie nodded as Nancy went to see what her mom wanted.

Mom looked up from her position at the counter where she'd taken over making the salad. "I'll clear out my stuff after dinner and change the sheets before I go."

"You sure?" She didn't want her mom to feel like she was being kicked to the curb.

"I was only here for one reason."

"You trust her to watch my back?"

"If Carter does then I do. That man cares too much about you to put you in less than capable hands. I have no doubt he'd camp out here himself if he didn't have his nephew."

Nancy opened her mouth to argue about Carter's feelings but snapped it shut at the don't-argue-with-me look on her mom's face. "I'll set the table."

A short time later, the three ladies sat around the table. Mom offered a blessing for the food, then they dug in.

Jessie raised her fork. "Carter filled me in on everything that's going on, and I must say, I'm surprised at how calm you are about your situation, Nancy."

"Stressing won't do any good. Rather it will tire me out and weaken my defenses. I choose to trust the Lord that everything will turn out in the end."

Annoyance covered Jessie's face. "He's not your fairy godfather."

"I didn't suggest He was." Clearly God was a touchy subject with her bodyguard. "I was only acknowledging my faith in Him and that I trust Him to take care of me. I also believe He expects me to use all the resources available to me to stay safe."

Mom's gaze went from Nancy to their guest. "What brings you to Tipton, Jessie?"

"Carter said you're the sheriff, otherwise I would sidestep your question. I shot a man in the line of duty. He pulled a gun from his pocket. I shot first. I'm alive, and he's not."

"You're on administrative leave while the incident is under investigation. Seems pretty cut and dry."

Jessie nodded. "I've been cleared and am taking some personal time." She looked to Nancy. "We need to go over ground rules on how this is going to work. I'm told you work at the public library, and that there's one main exit and two emergency exits."

Nancy nodded. "I have one assistant and there can be up to twenty people at a time there, but generally it's not that busy."

Relief shone on Jessie's face. "That's a lot better than what I'd imagined. I'd like to go over early to get a feel for the layout and make any necessary changes."

"Changes?" Nancy squeaked.

"Don't worry. I'll try to make my suggestions as painless as possible." She turned her attention to Sheriff Daley. "Who do you like for the person threatening Nancy?"

"I'm at a loss. We've followed up on leads, but they turned out to be dead ends. I've had one of my deputies keep a close eye on Nancy, but he hasn't spotted anyone following her or paying any special attention to her. That has only happened when she's been alone. I'm glad she'll have a shadow. Now we can focus all our resources on finding and apprehending this person. We're assuming the license plate thefts are related to the threats made to Nancy."

"Right. Carter brought me up to speed, but what about the home burglaries? Any connection there?"

"Not that we've been able to discover. We've had a lot of newcomers in the county this past year. Crime has risen county-wide. There was a weapons stash at a storage unit in Payton, but it appears to be unrelated."

Jessie nodded and took another bite.

Nancy shifted in her seat. "Please excuse me. I'm going to prepare your room."

"I said I would." Mom started to rise.

Nancy motioned her down. "You made dinner. The two of you can talk shop." She fled the room before Mom had a chance to argue. As grateful as she was to her mom and the entire department, she was weary of people being around all the time and having to constantly watch over her shoulder. This needed to end.

# Chapter Nineteen

IF JESSIE THOUGHT SHE COULD COME into the library and start rearranging furniture she had another think coming. "I understand your concern, but as I explained earlier, my desk is a permanent fixture. It's impossible to move."

Jessie's brow furrowed. "You're too exposed in the middle of the floor space. You're accessible from every direction." She rested her hands on her hips. "What about moving to a temporary station against the wall beside the emergency exit?"

"I need to be in the center of the library near the front so I can keep an eye on things and check out books for people."

"You're not making this easy." Jessie raised her hand and tucked a few loose strands of hair behind her ear.

"I'm sorry. The things that have happened have been scare tactics. I've never been physically harmed."

"Yet. There's a pattern of escalation. We can't be too careful."

The front door slid open, and Tara walked in. "Good morning!" She smiled brightly.

"Hi." Nancy shot a questioning look toward Jessie. Could she tell Tara who the woman was?

Jessie shook her head slightly.

"Tara, this is Jessie. She's a friend of Carter's, and she's staying with me for a few days."

"Welcome to Tipton. This is a great little town."

"Thanks. Have you lived here long?" Jessie asked.

"I'm a relative newcomer. I saw the listing for this job online. I've always loved the idea of small town life, so when the job was offered to me I jumped at the chance. What brings you to Tipton?"

"Carter is a good friend. I'm on vacation and wanted to see him."

"Oh." Tara shot a concerned look toward Nancy.

Nancy smiled. "It's fine. We're all friends."

Tara raised a brow. "Okay then. I have work to do. It was nice meeting you, Jessie."

"Likewise."

Nancy hadn't anticipated the need to keep Jessie's purpose for being there from Tara. How would she explain the woman's presence if she was there constantly? She glanced toward Jessie who seemed to be contemplating how she would get her way with the setup of Nancy's workstation. Nancy squared her shoulders and raised her chin. "I appreciate what you're doing, and I know I agreed to this, but moving my desk is non-negotiable. I'm sorry."

Jessie nodded, seeming to accept the new terms. "Fine. But it will make my job easier if you'll stay in one place as much as possible."

"Since Tara is here, that's not a problem." She situated herself behind her desk and got to work, doing her best to ignore Jessie who sat nearby with a magazine in her lap. Time passed slowly, but at least she was getting some work accomplished.

Around eleven, Tara sidled up to Nancy then squatted beside her and whispered. "What's with Jessie? Why is she spending her vacation in the library?"

"She asked to hang out with me at the library while Carter is working."

Tara frowned. "She's a grown woman. She can't entertain herself?"

"I don't judge and neither should you."

Tara huffed a breath and stood. "When will you be taking lunch? I'd like to take mine at twelve-thirty."

Nancy checked the time. "It's almost eleven now. I suppose we'll head out at the top of the hour." They'd avoid the lunch rush and be back in plenty of time to relieve Tara.

"Perfect. Normally I wouldn't mind, but I have a haircut appointment."

Nancy nodded then turned her attention to a patron who wanted to check out a book. The next fifteen minutes flew by. She stood, grabbed her coat and purse, then headed for the exit. Jessie met her at the door and they left together.

Once outside she breathed easier. What was it about the library of late? She hadn't realized how tense she'd been until she left the building.

"Where are we going?" Jessie walked somewhat beside her, but hanging back a step.

"Daisy's Diner. It's about a block away on the left. The food is fresh and locally sourced. You'll love it."

"Sounds good to me."

A few minutes later, Nancy pushed into her favorite lunch spot and found a seat along the rear wall. "Order whatever you want, my treat."

"That's not necessary, but thank you."

"It's the least I can do, considering."

Jessie seemed to accept her argument and studied the menu. A short time later they placed their orders.

Jessie's gaze constantly roved around the diner. "The people here are staring at me," she whispered through barely moving lips.

"Sorry about that." Nancy stood. "Everyone, meet Jessie." She turned to Jessie then motioned to the other patrons. "Jessie. Everyone. She's visiting Deputy Malone from L.A. and crashing at my place. She's my sidekick while the deputy is on duty." She sat back down. "That should take care of them." She chuckled at the look of shock on her bodyguard's face.

Jessie's cheeks had turned bright pink. "I can't believe you did that."

Nancy looked over her shoulder and noted everyone had returned to their own business. "It worked. See? They were only curious about you. Now that they know who you are, it's all good."

She shook her head. "What can you tell me about Tara?"

"She lives alone, she's a good employee, always on time, and does her job the way I ask." Nancy tapped her fingers on the tabletop. "She took a few weeks off this fall to take care of her sick mother."

Jessie nodded. "Do you trust her?"

"Yes. As much as I trust anyone."

Her eyebrows rose.

"What?"

"Nothing, except Carter told me you have trust issues."

Nancy's mouth opened, then she snapped it shut. She should have expected he would tell his friend about her, but of all the things he could say, why that?

"I see the wheels of your mind churning. Don't worry, he didn't spill your life secrets. I needed basic information about you."

Nancy nodded. "I guess that makes sense." She twirled the straw in her water glass. "What else did he say?"

Jessie laughed, then quickly sobered. "A professional-looking woman, with long straight hair is heading our way." She kept her tone even, but Nancy heard the tension.

She glanced over her shoulder and waved. "Hi, Lilly."

The real estate agent smiled and slowed to a stop beside their table. "I hear we have a newcomer." She held out her hand. "I'm Lilly Prescott, Tipton's local real estate agent." She handed Jessie her business card. "If you find yourself in need of accommodations, give me a call. I can help you find a rental or make that all important purchase."

Nancy resisted rolling her eyes. "She's not moving to Tipton, Lilly."

The woman smiled brighter. "You never know." She turned and strolled to a table near the door.

"Well, all righty. That was...unusual."

Nancy chuckled. "Even for Tipton." She glanced over her shoulder. What had come over Lilly? That was weird.

"What can you tell me about her?"

Their Cobb salads arrived. Nancy shrugged. "Not a lot. She's lived here her whole life. We don't run in the same circle. She's a divorcee trying to make a success of her life. I guess she's learned to be aggressive to get what she wants."

"Hmm." Jessie forked a bite of her salad and chewed thoughtfully. "What time do you need to be back?"

"No later than twelve thirty, but technically I need to return to work by noon. Why?"

"Thought it'd be fun to walk through town and see who turns up." She took another bite then motioned to Nancy to hurry up and eat.

What was Jessie up to?

Carter sat on his couch, watching Jessie pace his living room, deep in thought. Nancy, Maddie, and Gavin were in the kitchen baking cookies for the teens' book club. He'd go and help them, but Jessie's pacing meant one thing—she was onto something but still working out the details.

She stopped and plopped onto the chair facing him. "I've watched her for two days as people come and go from the library. The people in this town are very friendly."

He grinned. "One of the first things I noticed. What do you have, Jess?" He kept his voice low.

"Her inner circle is limited, and from what I can tell, safe. Tara gives me pause, but she doesn't raise any flags."

"I felt the same."

"Interesting. Her next ring of people leaves things wide open. There are the people at the diner, her friend at the coffee shop."

"You mean Pepper?"

She pulled a pad from her pocket and flipped through it, then looked up. "Yes."

He nodded. "Go on."

"Everyone treats her like she's their best friend or

family. This town thinks very highly of Nancy."

"Agreed. So where does that leave us?"

"I don't know. Something feels off at the library, but I can't put my finger on it. Nancy's tense there."

He nodded. "Any idea why?"

She shook her head. "She appears to get along with everyone, so it doesn't make sense."

"She mentioned feeling like she's being watched when she's there."

"That could explain it, but I haven't noticed anyone paying special attention to her."

He'd had the same impression. Whoever was behind the notes was very good at remaining invisible. He sighed. "I'd hoped you would be able to see something we'd missed."

"I'm sorry. On the bright side, there haven't been any new threats made against her, and based on what you said, there haven't been any license plates stolen in the past several days."

"True." What did that mean, though? Was the perp lying low or out of town or what?

"My leave time is about up. I'll need to head back to L.A. the day after tomorrow."

"I'm sorry I've kept you so busy you didn't get any of that R and R you talked about."

"Actually, this was a nice change of pace. For a small town, Tipton has a lot going on. I'm glad you landed here. You can be sure I'll be back. Maybe next time we can go hiking or something."

He grinned. "I'd like that." Does Nancy hike? He'd have to ask her. It'd be fun to take a group over to the Sister's Wilderness in Central Oregon.

Jessie stood. "Think I'll join the bakers. Maybe

they'll even let me sample a cookie." She strolled from the room.

Lacing his fingers behind his head, Carter leaned back. Being here like this with Gavin and the girls felt right. For the first time in a long while he was truly content—at least on a personal level. Professionally he was stumped, and that ate at him.

Movement caught his eye, and he blinked, clearing his vision. Nancy held a plate of cookies. "Would you like one? They're chocolate chip."

He reached out and took two. "They're still warm."

"It'd be a crime to offer you a cold one. I wouldn't want you to haul me to jail again."

He grinned and took a bite. It melted in his mouth. "Had I known you could bake like this I never would have arrested you."

She laughed. "Liar."

He chuckled, thankful that they could banter so easily now.

"This has been fun, but I should head home."

"Don't leave without Jessie."

"I heard my name." Jessie ambled into the room.

"I need to go home." Nancy shrugged into her coat.

Carter stood, walked the women to the door, and watched as they left. A sense of loss washed over him. Nancy had wiggled her way into his heart, but there was nothing he could do about it—yet.

# Chapter Twenty

NANCY AWOKE TO THE BUZZING OF her phone. She checked the clock—midnight. Her pulse amped. She reached over and answered without checking the caller I.D. "Hello," she said softly since Jessie slept in the room across the hall.

"Miss Daley?"

Alarm shot through Nancy. She sat up. "Maddie? What's wrong?"

"I'm downtown, and I saw something."

Nancy's pulse thrummed in her ears.

"What did you see?"

"A woman wearing a hoodie matching the description of the license plate thief is down here. She looks like she's waiting to meet someone."

Nancy kicked off the covers and in seconds had tossed on a pair of jeans, a T-shirt, socks, and shoes. She rushed to the front door, grabbed her jacket and slipped outside. "Sweetie, are you in a safe place?"

"I think so. What should I do?"

"Call 911 and stay out of sight. I'm on my way to you. Where are you?"

"I'm by the library. I was sitting on the bench when I saw someone approaching so I snuck around the corner."

"Okay. I'll be there in a jiffy. Hang tight. I'll call you back when I get there." She raced to her car. Her engine was loud. They'd hear her coming. She'd have to take the risk, but park a block or two away.

She hit the gas and zoomed toward downtown. Halfway there she remembered Jessie and groaned. Her bodyguard would not be happy with her, but she'd call as soon as she parked.

The library came into view. Nancy pulled over and sent a text to Jessie then got out and stepped into the shadows. She needed to assess the situation at the library. She jetted across the street and crept to a good position. She drew her cell phone from her pocket and called Maddie.

"Hello?" The girl's voice shook.

"It's me, Maddie." She took a breath and tried to let it out slowly. "Where are you? Did you call 911? Are the cops on their way?"

"Run, Miss—!"

Nancy raced across the street toward the library with the phone to her ear.

"You're not as smart as I thought." A familiar female voice spoke into Maddie's phone.

"Who is this, and what did you do to Maddie?"

"She's fine, but you won't be."

Nancy stopped at the statues and crouched low. Movement near the street grabbed her attention. Was that Gavin? What was he doing here? "Who is this?" she demanded again.

"Oh no. I want to see your face when you find out that you aren't the sleuth you thought you were."

"Where are you? Why are you doing this?"

"Don't you wish you knew?"

Nancy gasped. She knew that voice.

Gavin drew closer.

Lilly stepped out from the shadows holding a gun to

Maddie's head. She pushed Maddie to the ground. "Tell that kid to scram and toss his phone so I can see it, unless he wants to meet his maker today. I don't want him calling the cops. I have some unfinished business with Nancy."

Nancy listened through the phone that Lilly had forgotten to disconnect.

"Gavin, you need to leave and throw your phone as far as you can then run!" Maddie shouted with a wobbly voice. She stayed on the ground where she'd fallen, as Gavin followed Lilly's instructions. Maddie's ankles were tied together, and her hands were bound in front of her with a zip tie.

"Stand up." Lilly waved the gun at Nancy.

She stood on shaky legs with her hands raised. "Let Maddie go. This can end now. No one's been hurt."

"Yet. But someone will be."

Nancy's focus jetted between Lilly and Maddie. At least the teen looked unharmed other than being shaken up.

Nancy swallowed the lump in her throat. "Why are you doing this?"

"I am sick of hearing about Tipton's darling. Nancy this and Nancy that. Blah, blah, blah." She paced and waved the gun in the air.

"This is about me? I don't understand how stealing license plates—"

"Of course you don't, Miss Perfect. You have no idea what it's like to be dumped aside and left to fend for yourself. I did what I had to do to survive. But then you had to meddle and poke around town. Don't even get me started on all the surveillance cameras you've forced me to avoid."

Nancy pressed her lips together. She didn't want to say anything to set Lilly off.

"Well?"

"Well what?" Nancy's voice came out breathless.

"What do you have to say? Surely the mighty Nancy Daley has questions."

Nancy swallowed the lump in her throat. If Lilly wanted to confess everything that probably meant she had no intention of letting them go. Surely Gavin went for help. "Okay. Did you steal the license plates?"

"Yes."

At Lilly's silence, Nancy realized the woman was waiting for more questions. "Why?"

She laughed. "Don't you wish you knew?" Lilly laughed again. "I love this. It's almost a shame I'm going to kill you, because it would be fun to think about you wondering day in and day out about the unsolvable mystery."

"If you don't want to tell me, then don't." As much as Nancy wanted to know, she knew this would irk Lilly. "I have another question, though." She spotted Carter across the street with Gavin and Jessie. Relief filled her, but this wasn't over yet. She needed to keep Lilly distracted. "Why do you hate me?"

"You really don't know, do you? I want what you have."

"Like what?" Nancy wasn't a rich woman, she'd been abandoned by her dad, she lived to work and had no contact with extended family. What was there to covet?

"The respect and admiration of everyone in this town."

"You have a funny way of trying to earn it."

"Shut up! You don't know me. You have no idea."

Nancy's arms hurt, and she lowered them slightly. "Then tell me."

"Too late. Time's up." She aimed the gun toward Nancy's head from about six feet away.

A shot rang out. Nancy dove to the ground.

"Stay here and call 911." Carter charged across the street, gun at the ready, leaving Jessie to call for backup. His heart raced. He'd hit his target but had the real estate agent got off a shot first? "Nancy! Maddie! Are you okay?" He stopped at Lilly's feet and checked her pulse—nothing. His stomach knotted. She wouldn't be moving any time soon. "It's over now. Are you hurt?"

Tears streamed down Maddie's face. "No. But Nancy's not moving."

He swung his attention to Nancy who still lay huddled in a ball. He didn't see any blood. Relief surged through him. He touched her shoulder. "Nancy."

She jumped.

"It's okay. I'm here, and no one is going to hurt you now."

Her eyes widened. She sat up. "What took you so long?"

He chuckled at the irritation in her voice. "I was a little late to the party. Are you okay?"

"I think she shot me." Nancy patted her body.

He wrapped an arm around her. "I don't think you were hit. You'd know it by now."

"Could you get me out of these zip ties?" Maddie held her hands out toward him.

He pulled a knife from his pocket and cut her free.

"Better?"

"Yes. Thanks."

"Come with me." He guided them to a bench nearby, but far enough away they wouldn't have to see Lilly's body. "I'll be back, but I need both of you to stay put."

Nancy nodded.

A siren sounded and grew louder by the second. Sheriff Daley's car squealed to a stop. He breathed easy for the first time since the alarm on his phone went off alerting him that someone had either entered or left the house. Once he realized Gavin was missing, he tracked his nephew's phone to downtown Tipton. Thankfully, he'd spotted Gavin right as he'd tossed his phone. An ambulance pulled up to the curb. He strode toward them.

The sheriff ran over to the bench where Nancy and Maddie sat. He'd join them as soon as the medics loaded up Lilly.

A few minutes later Sheriff Daley marched toward him. "Jessie filled me in, and Nancy told me the rest. Thanks for protecting her. One thing is eating at me though."

"What's that?"

"Ben Denson with Animal Control is still missing. Do you think he had anything to do with this?"

He shrugged. "It's hard to say."

"Is Lilly going to make it?"

He shook his head. The medics tried to revive her, but his shot had been fatal. "How's Nancy doing?"

"Best as can be expected. She's never been this close to danger. I don't understand any of this."

"I do." Maddie approached with Jessie and Gavin by her side, a protective look on his face.

"I asked you to stay across the street. This is a crime scene."

"And we are witnesses." Gavin raised his chin.

Jessie nodded.

"Actually, it's worse than that since Lilly held me hostage and made me call Nancy to lure her here."

"Sounds like there's a lot to sort out." Sheriff Daley motioned for him to take the kids over by Nancy. "I'll cordon off the scene. I've called in backup, and Lyle is on his way too."

Carter rested a hand on each of the teens' shoulders, guiding them to where Nancy waited. "Have a seat." He looked to Maddie. "Have you phoned your dad yet?"

Her eyes widened. "Do I have to?"

"No, but I think you should."

She sighed and made the call.

He turned his attention to his nephew. "I wish you would have trusted me enough to wake me up and tell me what was going on." Maybe then he could have diffused the situation before it went south.

"I'm sorry, Uncle Carter. It's not that I don't trust you. I didn't know what was going on or I would have. But I get now that I shouldn't have snuck out at all. I promise no matter what, I'll never do it again."

He patted his nephew's shoulder. "I'd sure appreciate that." Carter winced at the look on Maddie's face as she spoke with her dad. The girl had been through a lot by the sound of it, and now she had to deal with her dad too.

She pocketed her phone.

"Is he on his way?"

She nodded.

"Good." He pulled out his phone and pressed record. "You don't have to tell me anything without your dad here, but if you are willing, please tell me what happened. Start from the beginning, and don't leave anything out."

"I don't mind. I was out walking and spotted Lilly. I know her from when we bought our new house last year. I thought she was having car trouble when I saw her crouched behind one. Like maybe she had a flat or something, so I went up to her and offered to help." She looked to Gavin. "My dad taught me how to change a tire last year." She refocused her attention on Carter. "Anyway, I realized after it was too late what she was really doing. She grabbed me and told me if I knew what was good for me I'd cooperate. She told me to call Nancy and tell her I'd spotted the license plate thief and to sound scared. That part was easy, 'cause I was." She looked to Nancy. "I'm really sorry."

"It's okay. Everything turned out in the end. But keep going."

"She was acting crazy, like she was in need of a fix."

"You mean drugs?" Carter clarified.

"Yes. I didn't know she did drugs, but that's why she was stealing the plates. She said her supplier took the plates in exchange for painkillers."

"She was addicted to opioids?" Nancy stood and walked a couple of steps then back. "Did she name her supplier?"

"She kept mumbling something about a guy named Ben."

Nancy gasped, and her gaze slammed into Carter's. He wished he could decipher her thoughts.

"Apparently he was angry with her. He had a buyer

for a plate she hadn't delivered, and he was threatening to cut off her supply." Maddie grasped Gavin's hand. "That Ben guy sounded scary. She was really afraid of him."

This reminded him of his brother. Even Tipton hadn't escaped the clutches of the drug world. He came here to escape all of that and for a fresh start, but it seemed escape was impossible. "Where does Gavin fit into this?"

"I sent him a text about Lilly needing a tire change before I approached her. I pretended I didn't know how so he'd come keep me company." She ducked her head. "Sorry, Gavin."

He shrugged. "I'm glad you did, even if it was a lie. If you hadn't, then Nancy might be dead and tonight would have turned out a lot different."

"True," Carter said, noting the grim look on Jessie's face. He imagined she was frustrated with her protectee.

Nancy cleared her throat. "Did Lilly ever say how I'm involved? I still can't figure that part out."

"She really didn't like you. She kept saying something about her ex-husband and that it was your fault he left."

"I barely knew him. How is that possible?"

Maddie shrugged. "I had the impression her husband had a wandering eye. Nancy had caught it."

"I had no idea! I never had anything to do with her husband." Shock and disgust covered Nancy's face.

"It sounds like she was delusional," Carter said. "It'll take a while, but we'll get our answers. In the meantime, I believe that's your dad, Maddie."

Once Lyle cleared him, Luke Harms ran over to them. "What's going on, Maddie?"

"Mr. Harms, I'm Deputy Malone, Gavin's uncle. Your daughter spends a good deal of time at our place."

Her dad had a blank look on his face. Didn't Maddie tell him where she spent her time? "As you can see, your daughter is safe, but earlier she was held against her will at gun point."

Maddie's dad gasped, and he tugged his daughter close. "Was she kidnapped from our home? How could I have not known?"

"No, sir. She was walking downtown alone when she spotted a criminal we've been looking for."

"But I didn't know she was a criminal, Dad. Honest. I never would have approached her if I had."

"You approached a stranger in the middle of the night when you should have been at home in bed?"

"Well...she's not a stranger. She's our real estate agent."

"Ms. Prescott?" Shock echoed in his voice. Luke shook his head. "This is a lot to take in. Can my daughter leave now?"

"Do you have anything else to tell us, Maddie?" Carter still held his phone, recording everything.

"I think that's everything."

"Okay, then. If you think of anything else, please call me. You never know what information will help fill in the gaps."

She nodded, waved at Gavin, then walked away with her dad.

"Now what?" Nancy stood and tucked her hands into her jacket pockets.

"Now you let your mom and the others deal with this crime scene while Gavin and I walk you to your car then follow you home."

"Works for me. Not sure I'll sleep tonight, but home sounds wonderful."

He checked in with the sheriff then the three of them headed toward Nancy's house. There was a lot to sort through, but one thing still concerned him. Ben was on the loose, and since he'd reached out to Nancy, Carter was still afraid for her safety. This was going to be a long night.

# Chapter Twenty-One

"I DON'T UNDERSTAND WHY I HAVEN'T heard anything." Nancy peered out her living room window. Surely the police would have Ben in custody by now. She'd promised her mom she'd lay low and stay at home until they found him. That was three days ago. Jessie had to head back to California yesterday, and Nancy had been stir-crazy ever since.

Her phone rang. "Do you have him, Mom?"

"Yes. You can relax now. Ben Denson won't be bothering anyone for a long time."

Nancy blew out a long, slow breath. "Thanks for the call."

"You're welcome, sweetie. What are you going to do now?"

"I haven't thought that far ahead." Tiredness washed through her. "Maybe I'll take a nap. I haven't slept much the past few days." In truth, she wasn't sure how she was even standing.

"Sounds like a good idea, but you might want to get ready for a little company first."

"What are you talking about?"

"A certain someone was in a big rush to get out of here a moment ago."

"Oh! Okay, 'bye." Nancy rushed to her bedroom and threw on a long tunic and leggings, ran her fingers through her hair then touched up her face. Carter had sent several texts over the past few days. She hoped he was the visitor her mom was hinting at.

The doorbell pealed. Her heart pounded. She took a deep breath and let it out slowly before pulling the door open, smiling at Carter. "Hi."

"Hi, yourself. May I come in?"

"Of course." She stepped aside.

"Can I get you something to drink? Water, coffee, tea, hot chocolate?"

"Nothing, thanks. I've been given permission to fill you in on what we know."

Not exactly the romantic conversation she'd hoped to have, but she wouldn't complain. "Let's sit on the couch. I'm about dead on my feet." She tucked one leg under herself, and sat facing the opposite end of the couch.

Carter sat in the middle. "Ben was the owner of the storage unit we went to. It looks like he had a hand in more than just drugs."

"Why'd he stop paying the rent?"

"It appears he thought it was set to pay automatically out of an account he'd set up, but something went wrong. His mail was sent to a P.O. Box that he apparently never checked."

"Wow. What about the burglaries? Was he involved in those too?"

"Actually, no. He had Lilly doing that too. She had a serious addiction, and he was greedy. He kept upping the price until she had to resort to stealing. She traded her cache for drugs."

"I don't understand why he told me he found the owner of the snake. Why get involved at all with us when he was corrupt?"

"That's where the story gets interesting. According to Ben, Lilly had become a liability. He was afraid she'd say something to the wrong person, and his enterprise would go belly-up. By implicating her as the snake's owner, which she was, he was hoping she'd go away for a long time."

"Lilly put the snake in the library?"

Carter nodded. "She also started the fire with the smoke bomb."

"Why?"

"Ben said she'd become obsessed with you." He ducked his head. "Apparently she had a thing for me and felt like you were in the way."

Nancy gasped. "That explains so much." Her shoulders sagged. "I'm glad this is over, and life can return to normal. I don't know how you do this all day every day. I'm exhausted."

He chuckled. "I predict you'll be back to your sleuthing ways by this time next week."

She grinned. "You might be right."

"Oh, I know I'm right." He winked. "But there's one thing I don't know."

"What's that?" Hadn't they covered everything?

"If you'll go to dinner with me on a real date."

A warm feeling washed through her. She tilted her head. "Well, I don't know."

His eyes widened.

"Just kidding. I'd love to have dinner with you."

"There's no time like the present."

She grinned. Who needed sleep? "Sounds like a good plan to me."

He stood, reached for her hand then pulled her up. They were so close she could feel his breath on her face. He leaned closer. She closed her eyes as his soft lips brushed hers. "Will all our dates start like this?" She asked softly.

"I sure hope so." He kissed her again—thoroughly this time.

# Now, a Sneak Peek at
# Book Two—The Sleuth's Dilemma

## Chapter One

ANNA PLUM TRIED NOT TO FIDGET in her seat. She hated meetings, and this one in particular made her uneasy. She glanced at her co-workers, Luke Harms and Stan Gibson, who were seated around the conference room table. Why had Titus Gains, Tipton High School's newest guidance counselor, asked the English teachers to meet with him? In all the years she'd been teaching, a request like this had never come from a guidance counselor.

"Anna, I would like for you and Luke to co-chair this year's writing contest. Luke, you'll teach Anna the ropes?" Titus looked expectantly toward the department head.

Anna sat up from her slouched position and shot a look toward Luke. He was good at his job, but she dreaded working so closely with the man. "This is the first that I've heard I was stepping into this position. I'm not sure—"

Titus lifted a hand. "Sorry. From what I've been told the decision's been made. I'm only the messenger."

Anna's stomach sank. Luke was about as much fun

to work with as the Grinch at Christmas. He had no sense of humor and took life way too seriously.

Luke cleared his throat. "I've chaired the contest for the past five years and was promised by Ms. Porter I wouldn't have to do it anymore."

Anna had heard the principal had said as much, but for some reason hadn't given it a second thought. Too bad this hadn't come up sooner. Maybe then they could have avoided this awkward meeting.

Titus frowned and looked at his computer screen. "Right. I remember reading that in my notes from our faithful leader. She was hoping you would do it one last year, so you could train someone else to take over."

"I appreciate her position," Luke said. "But I really can't be bothered with it this year. I took on the advanced placement classes as well as college writing. The contest is a huge time drain. My classes would suffer, plus I'm in the middle of grading term papers. I wouldn't be able to give it, or Miss Plum, adequate attention."

Anna gasped. The nerve. As if she needed her hand held. She pulled her shoulders back and raised her chin.

Titus sighed.

Anna felt for him. It wasn't fair of their boss to thrust Titus into this position. He was, after all, a school counselor, not admin, but Ms. Porter, the principal, did things her own way, and since this was the only high school in town, Anna had learned to grin and bear it, whether she agreed with a decision or not.

"Right. I forgot the reason behind you not chairing it this year. Give me a minute to re-read my notes." A couple minutes later he looked up. "You're off the hook this year, Luke. Anna, that leaves you and Stan."

"Works for me." She grinned at Titus then shot a scathing look toward the English department head. The man was so oblivious he didn't even notice. Stan was fresh out of college and his enthusiasm for teaching was inspiring.

Titus sent Anna a smile that would make a movie star jealous. His flawless teeth, strong, clean-shaven jawline, and thick dark hair were perfect enough to grace the cover of any magazine. How had he become a school counselor anyway? She pulled her attention away from the counselor and onto her least favorite teacher.

"Luke, I assume you don't mind being consulted if either of the newbies has a question?" A line etched between Titus's brows.

"I'll do my best." Luke shuffled through a file on the table in front of him.

"I'm sure Stan and I will be able to handle it without bothering you."

"Excellent." Titus shot her a half-smile. "That's all we had on the agenda today. Thanks, everyone."

Stan stood. "Anna, let's meet tomorrow after school to discuss our game plan. I need to take off right now."

"That's fine." It would give her time to dig up the rules from last year. The contest seemed to run itself when Luke was in charge. As much as she didn't like the man, she would give credit where it was due. "Luke, before you leave, can I get the contact information for the judges?"

He shook his head. "I'm afraid not."

She planted her hands on her hips. "Why?"

"I was the sole judge."

"You're kidding." How did he have the time? "No

wonder you don't want to keep chairing the contest. Is there a reason you did it yourself, or can I try and find judges?"

"I did it on my own because I couldn't find anyone to help." He raised a brow. "Including you, Miss Plum." He turned and strode from the room.

Anna gasped. "Of all the..."

A low slow whistle grabbed her attention.

She faced Titus and scowled.

"Sorry. The tension between you and Luke is palpable. Is there something I can do to help?"

She shook her head. "The man gets under my skin. That's all." Luke Harms used to be a great guy before his wife drowned, but ever since, he'd become difficult. She felt sorry for him, but at the same time he annoyed her more than anyone she'd ever met.

"I see. I hope the two of you can come to some sort of truce. I'd hate to see the English department fragmented."

She crossed her arms. "How is it you had the authority to let Luke out of co-chairing the contest?"

"I didn't. Ms. Porter had in her notes that if he threw a fit to give him his way, since she'd promised he wouldn't have to do it this year."

Her indignation fizzled. "Now it's my turn to apologize. I didn't mean to make your job more difficult than it already is."

"You're right. It hasn't been easy, but I like a challenge. Did you know I used to teach English Lit? If you decide to delegate and need judges, let me know. I'll take a stab at a few entries."

"Really?" Her voice rose in pitch. "That's so nice. Thanks."

"Sure. It could be fun." His deep, sky blue eyes twinkled.

Wow. How had she never noticed this man's beautiful eyes? Her heart beat wildly in her chest. "I... uh... should get out of here. My dog Freddy needs a walk and time to run."

He waved her ahead of him as they left the conference room. "What kind of dog is Freddy?"

"American Eskimo Spitz. He's a ball of white fur and loves nothing better than to run and play in the park." Her insides warmed thinking about her precious dog. She didn't know what she'd do without him. Freddy kept her warm at night and made her laugh when she was awake—at least when he wasn't into mischief, but even then he was often hilarious.

"I've seen those. They're cute. I have a chocolate Lab. Maybe we'll see you at the park one of these days."

"Not likely with the hours you keep."

He sobered and glanced her way. "I need to work on my priorities. My first year here has been a challenge, but I feel like I know most everyone at the school now, and I'm getting the hang of how things are done." He continued walking toward his office, which was in the same direction Anna was heading.

"I'm glad. The students seem to really like you. But what's not to like?" Her face heated. "Sorry, I probably shouldn't have said that last part." She couldn't even look him in the eyes.

He chuckled. "No worries. I'll take the compliment."

Relief washed over her, and she grinned. "I'll see you tomorrow."

Titus parked his pickup along the street near Tipton Park. Rudy, his two-year-old Labrador retriever barked.

"Hold on." He got out and patted his leg. "Come on, boy."

Rudy leapt from the cab of his pickup and danced in a circle.

Titus laughed. He closed and locked the door then jogged toward a grassy knoll. Rudy loped ahead of him a few feet. Anna's mention of her dog needing exercise reminded him it had been a while since he'd brought Rudy to a park. He tossed the ball he'd brought, and Rudy tore after it.

Titus looked around, taking in the green space. Cherry blossom buds colored the trees. Young mothers watched their little ones climb on the play equipment that would rival the playgrounds in a city twice the size of Tipton. Rudy bounded toward him and dropped the ball at his feet. "Good boy." He grabbed the ball and tossed it again.

"Well, this is a surprise."

He turned and saw Anna strolling toward him with a white ball of fluff on a leash. "I'll say. This must be Freddy."

Anna grinned, and her eyes widened. "You remember names better than you let on."

Rudy slid to a stop and dropped the ball. Then he noticed Freddy and moved close for a sniff and greet.

Anna watched the dogs closely. "They seem to like each other." She reached down and unhooked Freddy's leash. "Hopefully this little guy won't run off. I can't tell you how many times I've had to chase after him." She tossed Freddy's ball. "Here's to hoping."

Titus threw Rudy's ball too, and both dogs tore after the toys. "Have you made any progress on the writing contest?" He glanced her way, but kept his attention focused on the dogs.

"Not much. I printed off last year's rules. Fortunately, the deadline and rules were already posted on the school's website. So now it's only a matter of judging."

"I'm really sorry about how all of this was dumped on you. Apparently, Ms. Porter had forgotten that she'd promised Luke he didn't have to do it this year. She'd hoped he would help train you, but we know how that turned out. I suggested skipping it, but apparently this contest is a huge deal to a lot of the students."

"It is, and I wouldn't want to see it go away, but I sure wish I hadn't had that contest dropped on me at the last minute. I feel so behind already. There's so much that I should've been doing in preparation, but now I have to wing it. Not my favorite way of doing things." Anna looked wistfully toward the dogs as they trotted back to them.

"I would imagine not. If there was any other option..."

Anna shook her head. "Sorry, I know it's not your fault. I won't complain again. I promise." She crossed her heart with her pointer finger.

He chuckled. "Relax, Anna. I don't mind a little venting. I wasn't all that happy when I was told I had to run the meeting. It doesn't fall under my job description."

"I'm afraid Ms. Porter is like that. You'll get used to the way she does things."

The dogs lost interest in chasing their balls and began to follow their noses around the park. "Think we should trail them?"

"Probably." She sauntered after the animals.

He kept pace. "Tell me about Tipton."

She shot him a startled look. "You've lived here since August, haven't you? That was seven months ago."

He nodded. "I don't get out much."

"What do you want to know?"

He shrugged. "Anything. I've been married to my work, and other than trips to the grocery store and coffee shop, I haven't been out. What do people do here for fun? Where's the best place to eat?"

"Hmm. Well, it depends on the time of year. At Christmastime, there's the annual tree lighting and Christmas caroling around the tree along with hot chocolate and cookies. But the spring is iffy, as I'm sure you've noticed. The cherry blossom festival was cancelled due to lack of funding. In the summer months, there's a movie in the park on Friday nights. That's always a hit. And in the fall, there's a harvest festival. You didn't go to that?" She glanced his way.

"I'm afraid not. Like I said, I've been immersed in work. But I've noticed the people here are friendly—at least they are now." He chuckled. "When I first arrived, it was awkward."

"What do you mean?" Anna whistled. Freddy looked up then trotted their direction.

"The day I arrived here I went to Roaster's Coffee, and everyone stopped what they were doing to stare at me."

She sighed. "What did you do?"

"I figured they were probably curious, so I

introduced myself as the guidance counselor at the high school."

"That was smart." Admiration filled her voice. "Then what happened?"

"Everyone went back to their business, and the owner of the place gave me a coffee and donut on the house as a welcome to town."

"That sounds like Pepper."

He wouldn't know, and to his shame, he had assumed she was hitting on him. Guess not. His face heated. He cleared his throat. "So how long have you been teaching at the high school?"

"This was my first job after graduating with my masters."

He'd do the math if he had a clue how old she was. "So that makes what, five years?"

She laughed. "I knew I liked you. Sure, let's say five." Freddy leaned against her leg and looked up at her. "Looks like he's ready to head home."

"Yeah, I suppose Rudy is too." They walked toward the sidewalk. "Guess, I'll see you at work."

She nodded. "You asked about places to eat. Pretty much anyplace in town is good, but Daisy's Diner is a favorite of mine because they use fresh ingredients. Daisy grows them year-round in her greenhouse and garden."

"Thanks for the tip." He unlocked his pickup and noted Anna kept walking. "Did you drive here?"

She turned back to face him. "We walked. Normally my neighbor and I walk together, but she couldn't today."

"Would you like a ride?"

"Thanks, but it's so nice, I'd rather walk."

He nodded. Anna was an interesting lady. He'd like to get to know her better, but he had to walk a fine line. He enjoyed his job and didn't want to do anything to jeopardize it. Besides, he'd heard through the grapevine that Anna didn't date—another thing they had in common. He knew why he didn't date, but why didn't Anna?

# Author Notes

Tipton is a fictional town placed in the Willamette Valley near Salem. I love setting stories in fictional small towns because it gives me creative license to do anything I want. I hope you enjoyed the result.

The next book in this series will continue to follow Nancy as well as Anna.

LINKS

Subscribe to Kimberly's newsletter to learn about upcoming releases, sales, and to simply stay in contact: http://www.kimberlyrjohnson.com/

Join Kimberly on Facebook:
https://www.facebook.com/KimberlyRoseJohnson

Follow Kimberly on Amazon: http://amzn.to/2jArIFU

Follow Kimberly on BookBub:
https://www.bookbub.com/authors/kimberly-rose-johnson

# Books by Kimberly Rose Johnson

## Brides of Seattle
The Reluctant Groom
Melodies of Love
A Love Song for Kayla
An Encore for Estelle
A Waltz for Amber

## Sunriver Dreams
A Love to Treasure
A Christmas Homecoming
Designing Love

## Wildflower B&B Romance Series
Island Refuge
Island Dreams
Island Christmas
Island Hope

## Contemporary Inspirational Romance Collection
In Love and War
Contemporary Novella
Brewed with Love

Made in the USA
Monee, IL
29 August 2023

41806699R00125